"Don't go near him!" Captain Gibson bellowed, emerging from his lair. He recognised the symptoms of nerve agent poisoning, and knew that everyone was in danger. "Melia, form a cordon," he ordered her. "We need HazMat!"

Mellors saw an opportunity to be useful and directed all the other volunteers to ditch their tools, just in case. They piled them in the centre of the space. Everyone was worried, scared that they might have picked up something deadly.

An ambulance arrived and the paramedics were wearing protective gear. They had a trolley with them. They loaded Mr Cyril Corsh on board and wheeled him up the slope, with interested parties following on, chattering and looking anxious. Melia was in the throng. They arrived at the Manor House, and a helicopter was waiting in front, on the lawn.

"Thank Goodness for Air Ambulance," Melia remarked to Marilyn, who was standing there, looking on.

"Oh, that's Mr Corsh's own helicopter," Marilyn assured Melia pointedly.

She would recognise it anywhere.

ACKNOWLEDGEMENTS

Cover: by Mike Ather, 'Zodiac Film'
Other books by this author:
are available
(in the 'Mickey from Manchester' series).
And 'Amelia Hartliss Mysteries', the series.
(A full list of these publications
is at the back of this book.
And if you make it that far,
well, we're all impressed..
Well done.)

TITLE

Tales Of Old
Buile Hill
A Crime Fiction Thriller
by
Mike Scantlebury

The 'Amelia Hartliss Mysteries' series, Book 25

Published in Britain the second year of Covid, as part of
National Novel Writing Month 2021

COPYRIGHT

DEDICATION

This book came to be written in the cold, dark days of November 2021, when the world was grimly facing a second long hard winter of pandemic, infection and separation.
As Christmas appeared as a merry mirage on the horizon, our thoughts all turned to the elves and pixies, ghosts and phantoms that come out from Halloween to New Year's Eve.
Solstice seemed like a meaningless stop along the never-ending road of misery.
The spirit world makes occasional interruptions in this story, and you, the Reader, are urged to consider a wider tradition in British culture - the world of Pantomime, where folk tales are interspersed with scenes from the present day and songs from the present.
How crazy is that? This mixture here is no less a melange and no more logical or believable.
On the other hand, you can make up your own mind.

CHAPTER ONE: Long Boxes

Melia was cold. She was wet. She was very unhappy.

It was the middle of the night and she was sitting in a car with a colleague from work. It didn't help that he seemed happier than normal, but that was Terry. He didn't leave the office much, and this was a treat for him.

He called it 'a Stakeout'.

"You've been watching too much television," Melia told him.

Terry looked baffled.

"I don't own a TV," he replied. "I watch Catch-up and Box Sets on my laptop computer. Why would I need a big screen?"

That was a very modern thing to say, Melia reflected. But that was Terry. He was younger than her, a computer nerd. With his flyaway ginger hair and thick spectacles, he simply looked the part. He was the 'go-to' guy in the office, the one who solved everyone else's problems with their computers. He didn't belong here.

Here? They were outside the front of the old Manor House, at the top of the hill in Buile Hill park. Well, strictly speaking, it was on their left. They were parked with the back of the car up against a tree. On their right was the Conference Centre - the place for weddings, business get-togethers and dances. Built in the 1930s, it was a squat, low building, that seemed to stretch forever back into the gloomy night. Strangely, there was an extra floor above the dance-floor area and there seemed to be lights on. That was a mystery, Melia was thinking. After all, nobody lived there.

Nobody lived in the Manor House either. Now. It had once been a grand house, when the area was privately owned, but what was now the park had been given to the people of Salford in the early years of the 20th century, at a point when the gentry who lived in the building could no longer afford their extravagant lifestyle. The place had been turned into a Museum for a long time, local residents said to Melia, but then the Council had found that it was too expensive to maintain, so they boarded the place up and left it to wait for better times. A shame. It was a sound-looking, stone pile, with an impressive pediment and front door. It had three stories and a cupola on top. There was a wing on the right, but no windows. It would have been really busy in Victorian days, she was thinking, with the servants bustling and the Lords and Ladies arriving in their horse-drawn carriages.

Melia, she said to herself, you have been watching too much television too. All your fantasies are coming from that box. This is just a run-down ruin in the middle of Salford, a run-down town in the middle of the North West of England. Stop creating fairy stories, she thought to herself.

It's a city, she corrected herself, grumpily. A city. Not a town.

She was sitting in the driving seat. She reached up a hand and looked at herself in the rear view mirror. She was wearing a thick, woollen cap and her long hair had been scrunched up inside it. No make-up, and a scarf around her throat. She had her regular leather jacket, but with two thin sweaters under that, over her shirt, with thick jeans, to keep out the cold. She didn't look a fraction like her usual glamorous self, which was one depressing thing, but at least she had wrapped up warm for her night in the car.

Terry had gone one further, bringing his own home-made sandwiches in a plastic box and a flask of hot coffee. That was fine, until he passed her a cup of his home-brew and knocked it against the steering wheel, spilling the scalding coffee over Melia's knees. She yelled in protest and pain, wiping it away with her hand. She then demanded they have the car's heater on to dry her out, but Terry had baulked at that. He said they would draw attention to themselves. Melia looked out the window. It was past midnight, true, and the park was cold and deserted, true, but there were several cars parked along the grassy verge. She couldn't think why. Maybe people left them there for safety, not trusting their neighbours to let them park outside their own houses in safety. It was that kind of area, up there, north of the park. A little unsavoury, up towards Bolton Road. Mickey had considered living there, for a while, but then bought a mundane, semi-detached house on Bury New Road instead. She had stayed there recently, when she had her 'trouble', but she swept the thought aside.

No time for romance, she was thinking. This is work.

The 'work', the assignment she had been given, was to watch the Manor House and report if an illegal drug shipment arrived, to be stored there. That seemed an outlandish proposition on several levels. One, it was a deserted, empty house, but in the middle of a park? Hardly discrete. Second, her job rarely had anything to do with drugs. That would be the regular cops, surely. Captain Gibson smiled at her naiveté.

"We're talking Afghanistan," he said. "The Americans cleared out recently, in a hurry, and everything 'normal' has been suspended. The drug dealers could normally depend on the co-operation of local law enforcement and politicians, but they've all been swept away. Suddenly. So they've had to improvise. Our information is that every store in the country is being emptied and the contents flown out to any safe haven they can find. England is nearer than the USA. It might only be a stop-over, but high-grade opium is heading our way."

Melia had learned years ago to simply accept whatever the old man said. Her unit was a small fish in British Security, but the jobs it was given were usually vital. If her boss said it needed to be done, he was operating on orders from the highest level. Somebody in government wanted it done, and they turned to their 'go-to guy'.

And he had turned to her. She was his 'go-to' gal, she was thinking. She was the operative he could rely on. She did his dirty work, and never asked too many questions. Like now. Whatever was happening with the Manor House, she would find out eventually, of course. With her back-up, Terry.

Of course, Terry wasn't a Field Agent, but he had been there when orders were given and his eyes shone with excitement. He begged to be given the chance to ride along. Melia weighed it up. All they had to do was observe, she was thinking. So why not?

Spilling the coffee didn't help him him build his CV, of course, but a mistake was a mistake. She sighed. It wasn't helping.

Maybe if the pair had been forced to sit there all night, with nothing happening, Melia would have grown increasingly upset, but luckily, there were developments.

Quietly, with no lights, a large white van approached from the east, coming down the narrow track from the main road.

Melia and Terry scrunched down in their seats.

They were expecting it to stop at the front door - which was silly, because there were heavy boards across that entrance - and sure enough, the van continued, around the building and down the side. Fortunately, they were parked far enough along that the spies could actually see down that slight slope, between the old Manor House and the newer Conference Centre. The ground dropped away at that point, where the van stopped.

"If there's a side door, then it's to the cellars," Terry hissed, unnecessarily. Melia had come to the same conclusion.

Terry pulled out a pair of night vision goggles, then a small camera, and began snapping away at everything.

There were people in the front of the van, and when they stopped, they came out and moved around the back, opening the back doors. Two of them, wrapped up against the cold, with dark clothing and ski masks. These people, looking shifty, began unloading boxes and taking them in to the building, through a door that they somehow happened to be able to open. Long boxes, that the two men had to carry between them, one at each end.

"Coffins," Terry said, but again, Melia had her own goggles and could see that. Yes, coffins.

That was strange, she was thinking, but it made a lot of sense. If the Afghan gangs had been forced to smuggle a large quantity of drugs out of their collapsing country, what better disguise than coffins? Not many people would want to ask questions and open the boxes. Especially in the chaotic state the airport had been in, at the end. It had been an unmitigated disaster.

In the dim light on the inside of the van, the spies could see that there were many boxes, and unloading them was a long, slow, laborious process. Melia was thinking about counting them, but realised that Terry would be doing that. He was good with numbers. He was precise about everything.

"I'm going out," he said.

Melia automatically put a restraining hand on his arm, but then realised he was right. He needed some close-ups and also could catch the van in his sights on the way out. They weren't instructed to stop the villains. Observation, that was their responsibility. That was all. Observe, and report.

Terry waiting until the van people were inside the cellar, then carefully clicked the door open and slid out onto the grass. He went around the back of the car and hid behind another car, further along to the right. He would get good pictures there, Melia was thinking, and pushed down lower in her seat.

There was nothing for her to do. She relaxed a little and closed her eyes.

She snapped awake when there was the roar of an engine. The van had started up. It backed up, turned and started along the track, the way it had come. All over, Melia was thinking. Job done.

She let herself out of the car, stood up and stretched. Her knees were still wet, she noticed.

"Got the van, got the registration," Terry announced proudly, coming towards her.

Melia looked up. There were two of him.

She almost jumped out of her skin.

"Who is this?" she demanded, fighting to keep her voice low.

The second figure was taller than Terry. He was fully covered in ski mask, woolly hat, zipped up jacket. The lot.

"This is my pal Bais," Terry announced nonchalantly. "He's a colleague from the office. He brought his own car."

The man grunted, but obviously didn't see the necessity of an explanation, since Terry was vouching for him.

"A Back-up to your Back-up," Terry chuckled. "Don't worry, He'll be useful when we check the boxes."

Terry and the second man turned and started towards the side of the building.

Melia bridled, concerned that no one was following her orders. We shouldn't be doing this, she was thinking furiously. No need for further investigations. Just exactly who was in charge here?

By the time she caught up with the pair, Terry was working the lock on the side door. Melia looked up and down. Yes, it was an old wooden door, but dusty and rusted. It was let into the side wall at less than the main door level. A side entrance. For the servants, in olden days? It was easy to miss, easy to pass by and not notice when walking down the long hill, following the path from the trees.

Terry seemed to have come prepared. He had put down his rucksack beside him and taken out a battery light on an elastic strap, which he put on his head. He had a full set of skeleton keys and was jiggling the lock.

Something clicked.

"There, that wasn't so bad, was it?" he said, to no one in particular.

He opened the door and pushed inside. Melia followed on. She wasn't so hopeless: she had gloves, which she put on, and a torch, which she brought out of her own pocket. She brushed cobwebs aside and entered.

It was a long, stone-walled room. The coffins had been stacked on either side, from the floor, on top of each other, to waist height. Terry was running his fingers over the nearest one. It was surprisingly ornate, with brass handles and ridged strips along the top. Surely too good for the mere transit of dangerous drugs?

"It isn't locked," Terry said quietly. "None of them are locked." He eased the coffin open.

Melia jumped again. The box wasn't simply stacked with drugs. There was a body inside.

The old bald inhabitant was dressed in full military uniform and had rows of medals. A General?

"Clever," Terry said. "No mere Customs Officer is going to want to interfere with this."

The body was laid in plush velvet, padded so that he couldn't move around during travel.

"I need a knife," Terry said, talking to himself. "The Swiss Army knife, I think," he went on. "It's got scissors."

Before Melia could intervene, Terry had slashed the material and revealed what was underneath.

Plastic bags, dozens of them, crammed under the cover of the expensive cloth.

"They aren't white," Melia observed, wanting to be in on the discussion. "If it's drugs, it's white, right?"

"Clever," Terry said again. "This is unprocessed sludge. If it had been processed, then the total value would be in the millions, handy for any Customs person to help themselves to a bag or two, en route. But, unprocessed? It's worthless to anyone who hasn't got the equipment. You need a factory. Not everyone has that."

"Is every box the same?" Melia asked out loud, seeing Bais working his way down the line, checking.

Bais said: "You'll want to come and see this one. This one's not dead."

Chapter Two: Empty Sheds

Deputy Director Caulfield, Melia's boss, was having trouble with his new friends.

"You cannot expect me to climb that fence," he told them.

It was five o'clock in the morning in Buile Hill park, several hours after Melia had left the scene, and it was the other side of the Manor House, an area that might have been the stables when the place was occupied. In recent years it had been a Council Depot, active even when the big house had been boarded up and abandoned. Salford Council found a need for the old buildings, mainly using them to house their street sweepers and other practical vehicles, like the sit-on grass cutters that kept the parks of the city neat and tidy. There were a range of buildings in the compound, different shapes and sizes, including a little house that was used as offices, but then, suddenly and abruptly, this part of the old Buile Hill was given up too. The workers moved out, the vehicles moved elsewhere and a big padlock was put on the gate. The only visitors from then on were the local vandals, mostly young people, who had an interest in wrecking the place.

Like Mr Caulfield's gang.

They were there to 'state their case', they told him. To 'make a point'. The Council weren't listening to them, they said, so they would 'have to show them'. It didn't impress Caulfield. It was lawlessness, and, strictly speaking, he was an Officer of the Law. He hadn't told them that. He hadn't told them much about himself. He wasn't used to sharing.

Perhaps it was simply that he wasn't used to being in the position of having 'friends'. He had spent most of his middle-aged life knowing that most of the world hated him, and he had learned to live with that. He realised that he was happiest with himself when he could look in the mirror and know he was well dressed, in a smart suit, probably Italian, a flamboyant shirt and impressive tie. He liked himself like that. He didn't care what anyone else thought. He had reached middle-age with the belief that he didn't need other people, so he simply made sure he had the best haircut available, flicked back his hair and carried himself like a military man. Deep down he knew, although he wouldn't admit it, that all he really wanted in the world was to be Captain Gibson, the actual Director of the Unit, and deep down he feared - and it was a constant irritant - that he might never get to that height.

What did he do wrong, now? How did he get in this position?

He had made the mistake of moving house.

For years, ever since he moved to Britain from Australia, he had lived in a succession of nondescript flats, anonymous apartments that he preferred to be already furnished, so that he didn't even have to bother to think about what there was to sit on, or sleep on, or eat his breakfast on. But then Mickey had bought a house in North Salford, and he seemed so happy with it, gazing out of his front window onto the playing fields of Northumberland Street, up near Bury New Road. Caulfield realised that, since he was not in the habit of spending money unnecessarily, he had enough savings for a deposit on just such a suburban dwelling, and he strolled into a local Estate Agent and asked them what they had available to buy that day. He was directed to Strike Island.

It was an area he wasn't familiar with. Down by the river, on the opposite side to the University, the neighbourhood consisted mostly of what was once called 'Council Houses'. Built in the 1970s on land that had once been occupied by meagre terraced streets, with small houses, cheek by jowl, no gardens but a lively community atmosphere, the area had been completely cleared by Salford Council and replaced by smart new brick houses with tiny gardens at the front and back and room to park your car. Then, a decade later, the government of Mrs Thatcher had made the decision to make such rented property available for sale and slowly, house by house, street by street, the previous community spirit was whittled away and replaced by a more 'go-getter' attitude. The residents had been encouraged to show rugged individualism, and they took up the challenge in a rather aggressive way.

Caulfield encountered this tendency the first day he moved into his freshly painted house in Strike Island. There was a knock on the door and he opened up to find a number of his new neighbours standing there. In more amenable parts of the city, they might have presented him with a basket of fruit and a cheery smile. There were no smiles. They simply told him his presence was required at 'Dan's house', somewhat further along the street. Now.

Mr Caulfield made gentle efforts to demur, but his objections were swept aside. Thus, he found himself sitting in the corner of a rather threadbare sofa, offered a can of rather suspect lager beer, and forced to listen to a tirade against the supposed enemy, Salford Council. What had they done - apart from sell up their 'Social Housing', at the behest of central government in London?

They had caused the floods.

Caulfield rested his elbow on the side of the settee and found a place to rest his can beside it, on top of a pile of cardboard boxes, stacked full of more beer. So, these people had a hobby then, he reasoned, (and it wasn't healthy).

It meant they weren't that bothered about their own health, he could see. No, none of them were wearing masks, despite the fact that the pandemic was still running rife. They laughed in the face of a real threat to their health, it seemed, but appeared to be wound up about a supposed threat to their property from an overflowing River Irwell, just on their doorstep. They talked about a 'hundred year event', which should have meant any bad flood would only happen once in a hundred years, but it had happened last Christmas, they told him, and it might happen again.

When it did, several weeks later, Caulfield was unprepared.

He was roused from his bed by loud shouting from outside and banging on his door. He staggered downstairs in his dressing gown and was told to 'wrap up warm and grab a shovel'. Warmer clothes he had, a spade he didn't.

A few minutes later he was following the crowd to the end of the street, where he was astonished to see the river, lapping against the end house. That wasn't right! Water belonged in the river, not in people's houses.

"Grab those sandbags!" he was told, and the well-turned out and spruced up Mr Caulfield found himself part of a human chain, desperately trying to make a barrier against the rising tide.

This didn't seem right, he was thinking. Sure, it had been raining during the day, but seemingly no more than a usual Salford autumnal day. Where had all these flood-waters come from? More importantly, where were they going? Caulfield had read in a local newspaper that a new Flood Basin had been opened in this part of the city. The plan was that anything untoward coming down the river from Bolton or Bury would be diverted into it, (the old racecourse). It seemed like a foolproof plan to the Deputy Director.

Seemingly, it wasn't working?

In one of the short breaks allowed, when another neighbour from further up the street towards the landward side appeared with a tray of hot drinks, Caulfield tried to quiz the inhabitants.

What had gone wrong with the anti-flood precautions?

"You heard the siren?" one replied. "That's it. An early warning. That's the best they can give us."

Caulfield shook his head. There had been lots of sirens - there always was in this part of town. Which one in particular?

Later still, when they moved to the property next door and started adding sandbags to this next house in the line, Caulfield noticed some metal plates leaning against the wall, next to the front door. They seemed to be rusting.

When he enquired politely what they were for, the householder reacted angrily.

"They're meant to stop the water!" he snarled, and showed the Deputy Director how the thick metal was meant to slot into slides either side of the door and form a waterproof seal. It didn't work. The slider on one side was bent inwards.

How did that happen?

"The kids - " the man said vaguely.

So, the residents had been provided with some protection, but it wasn't maintained.

One of the other 'helpers', a tall man with reserved manners, pulled him to one side.

"After the last inundation," he whispered, trying not to be overheard, "I changed my front door. It's waterproof up to a metre and a half of water. Doesn't come cheap, mind. None of the rest of them would pay for such a thing."

No, Caulfield reflected, back in the cold and damp of an autumn morning, the sun not yet up. These people would rather join the 'Blame Culture' and choose somebody - in this case, the Council - or anybody, rather than admit that their future was in their own hands. It was more fun to have an enemy, he was thinking, knowing that he fulfilled that role for many of his colleagues down at Regional Office. He wasn't the 'Most Popular Man' in the Service.

"You don't have to climb the fence," a man in a mask announced, back in the present. "I've cut a hole in it."

The protesters piled through and spread out around the site to explore. The buildings were on a slope, down towards another fence, near the tennis courts. Some people went left and right, but Caulfield was drawn to a phalanx of the mob moving south, away from the gate. There, furthest point from the entrance, were the remains of several large greenhouses. The glass was long gone, but the timber frames were still standing, even though grass and weeds had grown from the floor to waist height.

"It's wood," one masked invader said, thrilled. "It will burn lovely."

Caulfield was outraged. The glasshouses were historic. They were well-made and would last another lifetime, if they could be restored. Why destroy them now? Just to upset the Councillors? What a total waste!

He leapt forward, about to argue his case, but a new development changed the need for that.

"Someone's coming!" someone shouted from the gate.

The interlopers sneaked back up the slope, keeping to the shadows, so as to not be seen. They bent over, trying to keep out of sight. What was going on? Caulfield heard the distinct sound of a diesel engine, revving hard.

Looking out through the fence, Caulfield was astonished to see a fuel tanker pull up to their left, towards the Manor House. It must have come into the park, passed them, gone down towards the Conference Centre and turned around. Now it was parked up, at the extreme left of the Depot. The driver leapt from his cab and started fussing with what looked like a derelict wooden cupboard on the wall. He opened the lid and revealed several large spigots.

"He's pumping gas!" somebody whispered, unnecessarily.

"I queued an hour to fill my car last week," another man said.

It was true. There had been a national shortage of petrol and diesel at filling stations in the last month. There had been a 'shortage of drivers', the television News told them. So what was this? The government could spare a few thousand gallons for an empty Depot? Where were the vehicles that needed to be filled?

Luckily the pumps of the tanker made sufficient noise to mask anything the fired-up residents were saying. It was certainly odd, Caulfield had to agree. The filling process went on and on. There must be a huge underground tank, he was thinking.

He felt a tap on his shoulder. Looking round, one of the most vocal of the contingent was beckoning him.

"Dave has got into one of the sheds," the man whispered, over his shoulder. "You need to look at this."

'Dave' had indeed broken a padlock and pulled back the door of a large building. It opened smoothly on a surprisingly well-oiled hinge. There was just enough light to make out a shape.

"It's a tank," Dave said.

Technically speaking, it's an armoured personnel carrier, Caulfield was thinking, but he didn't say.

"What's it doing here?" the two men asked, almost in unison.

Caulfield was appalled. Why was he the one who was expected to know? Had they guessed who he was?

Okay, he was employed by British Security, but looking at this - this thing - he had to admit, verbally and in his own head, he really had no idea what it was 'doing there'.

No. He didn't have a clue.

Chapter Three: Folk Tale

Once upon a time, deep in the woods on top of old Buile Hill, there lived a poor woodcutter, his wife and two children.

In many ways they were happy. The young boy and girl lived an idyllic life amongst the trees, playing with each other instead of going to school and watching their father work. But his life of cutting branches and creating charcoal was not enough to give the family the money they needed to survive. The woodcutter was ashamed to think that he could not support his family, and though he spent many sleepless nights lying awake, searching for ideas, he couldn't think of any way that he could improve his income and keep the family together.

Sometimes, when the children were asleep in their room, he woke, went into the kitchen and sat at the kitchen table in despair. He looked around their meagre rented cottage and tears came into his eyes. He could hardly afford to pay the rent to the owner abroad, let along pay for toys or amusements. The few things the children possessed were mostly made by his own hands - a wooden train and little painted lorry, a dolls' house and cradle amongst them. The clothes they walked around in were patched and repaired by his wife. The food they ate was supplemented by the roots and leaves he could find during his working day.

One dark night, when his wife woke up and joined him, they stared into each other's eyes and realised there was only one possible plan that would work. It was horrible to think, but, they concluded, they had no choice.

The next evening, the young children, the boy and the girl, were bathed and got ready for bed. Their father told them a fairy story as usual and tucked them in, then he and his wife sat at the kitchen table until they were asleep.

"Tonight?" he wife said, desperately. "Does it have to be tonight?"

The man nodded. It was a full moon. There would be light amongst the trees.

The woodcutter woke his children and told them to get dressed, then brought them into the kitchen and stood them in front of the fire, still glowing with the embers from the day.

"You are going on a great adventure," he told the little ones. "You must be brave, for all our sakes."

Then, taking their hands, he led them out of the cottage and into the deep, dark woods.

The man did not turn around. He knew his wife would be at the front door, tears on her cheeks. He knew he wouldn't have the strength to carry on, if he saw her there, so pathetic. He needed to be strong, to do what must be done.

"We are looking for elves and fairies," he whispered to his children. "When you find the tiny fairy folk, you will go and live with them. Your mother and I will love you always, but you must make a new life."

"Can we come and visit you, ever?" the little girl asked, close to tears.

"Of course you can," the answer came, "but your visits will be arranged by the magic people."

Plunging on along the narrow path through the woodland, they came into a moonlit grove. There was a tall man waiting for them, a man with a pointed hat. The woodcutter didn't know his name. The people around Buile Hill simply called him The Magus, the magic man. He was well known for his tricks and spells. He had great power.

"Two of them?" he asked, in a deep sonorous voice. He seemed mildly surprised.

The woodcutter nodded, knowing that he would get a better price.

The Magus reached into his cloak and brought out a roll of bills held together by an elastic band.

"The payment," he announced, "is as agreed. Do not dispute me now."

The woodcutter nodded, unable to argue.

He got down on his haunches so he could talk quietly to his children, for one last time.

"Go with this gentleman," he instructed them, "and do everything he says, exactly as he tells you to. He will raise you and educate you, and even teach you the lore of magic that he knows. Be brave."

"We will miss you, Father," the girl assured him.

"And I you," the woodcutter said. "Both of you, and in full. But our lives are different now. Everything must change."

He stood up, stood back and let the magic man direct his children away from the clearing. The youngsters turned and gave their Father one last small wave, but he was strong and didn't let them see that he was dying inside.

This is the worst thing I have ever done, he thought to himself, and cursed the Fates that had brought him to such an extreme. Still, he had a plan. He had the money now. He would use it, double it, then buy back his children and start a new life, maybe not in their run-down cottage, but far away, perhaps by the river, if they could afford the rent there.

The moon shone down and gave him the light he needed to find his way down the hill to the high road, on the level ground. He made good time, walking along the pavement towards the village. He had another meeting planned.

The Man was waiting for him, standing on the corner under an orange street-lamp. He gave no greeting, bar the nod of his covered head. He was wrapped warmly against the cold and wore a face-mask, to protect him from the plague.

"You have the money?" he hissed, and held out a wrinkled hand.

The woodcutter nodded, and handed him the paper money that he had been recently given.

The Man stared at it in irritation. He seemed unimpressed.

"For this amount, you get this amount," he said and held up a large clear plastic bag.

"Pills?" the woodcutter exploded. "I'm not used to the idea of pills. Haven't you got anything stronger?"

"They are all in little bags," he was told. "Each portion can be sold for double the money you pay for them."

The woodcutter was in no position to argue, not now, not ever. He was like a leaf tossed by the wind, blown amongst the brambles and over the tumps, settling anywhere and growing anew.

He watched The Man turn and limp off down the hill towards the docks. The woodcutter cursed him for his lack of feeling. The Man didn't care for anyone. Money was his drug, although he supplied other things to his many customers. He was a disgrace for a human being, but he had no need to fear: people needed him and what he had to offer. As long as they had those needs, he was their Master. No one was his superior, or his Lord.

The woodcutter set about his business. He walked down the other road, behind the shops, and came out on the highway to Liverpool. This was a main thoroughfare and a place he could meet people, people who may be interested in what he had to offer. They would be his customers, as he was to The Man. It was a chain.

He found the nearest tavern and plunged in, still shivering with the cold. He purchased a small beer with the few coins he had in his coat pocket and took it to a table at the back, against the wall. From there he had a good view of all the customers in tonight, and every person who entered. He was in the shadows, which was good, he reasoned, as he cut a strange figure in his heavy woodland overcoat and his thick boots. Still, once people worked their way along the bar they would see him there, and there would be no doubting his purpose. If they needed him, they would approach.

It was a quiet night, he observed. There were few people there already, and even so, two of them gave up on their evening out, stood up and left the premises. I need new arrivals, he was thinking to himself, and offered up a small prayer.

As if the angels had heard him, the main doors banged open and a gaggle of chattering young men burst into the small space. They looked neither hither or thither, as all their attention was on themselves. Still, one backed up against the bar. He turned, discerned its purpose and requested service. Drinks were served and money changed hands.

The woodcutter had his eyes on the man who paid. He didn't notice another, creeping towards him on the right.

"What have you got?" the kid asked arrogantly. His eyes stared, as if he was already drugged.

The woodcutter pulled a small clear bag from under his coat and offered it up to view.

"How much?" the kid hissed, looking as though he was intending to argue.

"It's good stuff," the seller insisted. "Take a sample. Give it a test."

"No need for that," the young man said, laughing abruptly. "There's five of us, give us a bag each."

The kids were talking at a table with seats off to the left, near the toilets. It would give the gang a chance to disappear from view if they needed to ingest, out of sight, the woodcutter was thinking.

The gang were giggling, though there was nothing amusing about the situation. They seemed to find each other the most gregarious company, and were thoroughly enjoying themselves. The woodcutter was worried. He was losing sight of the door. He didn't want to miss catching the eye of a potential customer. Maybe he should move, he was thinking.

There were plenty of hostelries along this stretch, he knew, each one full of possible buyers. He had been in this one single house for nearly an hour. It had been a good start, selling five bags, but he needed to sell them all, he knew.

His drink was finished and he needed the toilet.

Standing decisively, he pulled his coat around him and headed for the door marked 'Gents'. He passed the table of noisy young people, but they seemed to pay him no mind. Their attention was on other things.

It was a surprise, therefore, when he was washing his hands, to find that he was interrupted by the gang.

"How much money you got on you?" the lead kid demanded, and approached menacingly.

The woodcutter gaped. He only had the small amount they had given him.

There were five of them. They rushed him, and pinioned his arms to the wall. The front one went through the victim's pockets and found their money. He took it back, as if reclaiming stolen goods.

The woodcutter panicked. What if they stole his drugs? He needed those pills! They were his future.

In a sudden surge of strength he shook the smaller, younger men off, and backed up against the far wall.

"You can't do this!" he stated. "We did a trade. I gave you goods."

"But they're no good," the young man asserted, laughing at him.

The woodcutter stared. What? What were they saying?

"Pills?" the kid said scathingly. "Test them yourself. What do you think they are? What are they meant to do?"

"You're trying to cheat us," another one said.

"They're just sugar," a third said. "I haven't felt a thing."

"Trying to sell us fake merchandise?" the first one said slyly. "We should report you to the police."

It can't be, the woodcutter was thinking desperately. The Man had never let him down before.

"Give me the pills," he said. "Give them back. You can keep the money, but the pills - "

They took them out of their pockets and threw them at him, so that they spilled all over the floor.

"They're not worth anything, old man," the first guy said. "Don't bother picking them up."

"Wait," the second one said. "He tried to cheat us, right? He sold us fake stuff, and he was trying to leave. He thought he'd got away with it. We need to teach him a lesson. Maybe we should cut him. I've got a knife."

The woodcutter had an answer to that threat, at least. He reached into his belt and brought out one of the tools of his trade. The well-maintained and polished blade gleamed in the overhead lights, reflecting off the tiled walls.

"This is a knife," he said, through gritted teeth.

They left then, falling over themselves to get out. The door slammed and the old man was left alone.

Just as well. It meant that no one got to see the disappointment, the anger, the despair, in the woodcutter's eyes. He had taken a gamble on the lives of his children - and lost. Now he had no money, and no drugs to sell. He was even poorer than he had been before, having lost the only treasure he had left in his small and battered world.

Sliding slowly to the floor, he began to sob uncontrollably, for the first time in his adult life.

Chapter Four: Empty House

"I'm here to see the Mayor," the handsome young man said.

"My name is Marilyn," the pretty young woman told him. "I'm the Chair of 'The Friends of the Manor House', and we've organised this Open Day. As soon as the Mayor arrives, I'll be happy to introduce you. Do you have a particular question for him, or is there anything I can help you with?"

"I am Lord Turnton," he replied. "My family gave this building to the people of Salford in the early years of the twentieth century, before the First World War. Now I want it back. I want to know how soon the Mayor can arrange that."

Marilyn stood still, speechless and stunned.

Her little group was dedicated to restoring the Manor House to its former glory, then opening it up again for public use. They had no plans to give it away! This man - She had never seen him before. He was a stranger, and what he said -

She looked around at the festivities. There were tents and gazebos, laid out with tables of food and drink, and knick knacks to sell, to make money for her funds. It was a cold but bright Autumn day in Salford, with a chill in the air and the threat of a rain shower, but people seemed happy in their scarves and caps, wrapped up against the weather. They were circulating and chatting, stopping for a cup of tea or a cake. There were a lot of smiles.

This - this 'Lord' - would soon put a stop to that. If she told people -

In fact, that was to be a major part of the day. People had been invited to adjourn to the Conference Rooms next door, later in the afternoon, where the various competing ideas for what should happen to the grand old building would be laid out for scrutiny by the residents. The rich and affluent benefactors and philanthropists who had submitted their briefs to the Council had all been invited to give a short presentation, and stand on the low stage and answer questions from the floor. There had been a lot of rumours circulating in the city in the last year, and it had been Marilyn's bright idea to get it all out into the open. She hated the thought that the future of the Manor House might be decided behind closed doors, in some dreary Council Committee room, without any input from Salford people.

Without her.

The fact was that in the few short months she had been boss of 'The Friends' she had settled into the important role with gusto. She was having the time of her life. She was mixing with Mayors and Councillors, builders and planners. It was all so thrilling. She loved it. In fact, as she was loath to admit, if any plan went ahead and the restoration went ahead, she couldn't bear to think that she might then be redundant, not needed anymore.

She would have to think about that, she knew. She liked this life, and wanted it to continue.

As for Lord Turnton - the young man was impressed with the young woman called Marilyn. She was tall, she had long blonde hair and a full figure. She couldn't help remind him of a film star of the same name, long gone but still alive in the public consciousness. As he watched her moving about, talking to people, greeting new arrivals, he was impressed. She would make a worthy consort to any eligible bachelor, he was thinking. He knew he was good-looking, he had no modesty about that. They would make an impressive couple, he was thinking, should he ever consider marrying again.

"I'm Sol Senate," a deep, booming voice behind him announced. "I'm the elected Mayor of Salford."

Lord Turnton turned to face him.

The Mayor was as tall as him, but a little heavier with no sign of muscle. He had a completely bald head, as opposed to the Lord's flowing locks, but carried himself well. He seemed as confident in company as the Lord himself, although the Mayor had come from less impressive stock. Lord Turnton had been born important.

"I've been told you have a question for me," the Mayor said cheerily, unaware there might be a problem.

Lord Turnton decided he needed to come straight to the point.

"If you examine the Certificate of Gift carefully," he told the Mayor, lecturing, "you will see that my family donated this house to the people of Salford for their education and entertainment. However, if it was no longer required for any such thing, then it would revert to our possession. Now, as I understand it, it has been unused since the year 2000. That is coming up to 21 years, and that's the magic figure. The agreement clearly states 'twenty one years of disuse'. Mr Mayor, legally speaking, this building now belongs to me again."

The Mayor was shocked. He hadn't expected anything so confrontational. He took a breath.

"Isn't this something we can talk about?" he said quietly, knowing that losing the Manor House would be a devastating blow, not just to The Friends, but to all the voters in the city. It had been a fixture for so long, a jewel.

He said: "There's a few people with proposals coming this afternoon, We're going to go into the Conference Suite and hear them out. Perhaps you would like to put forward your plan then. Let the people decide."

"There's no 'decision'," Turnton said firmly, in his well-educated tones. "My 'plan' trumps everything, you might say."

I do believe you're right, the Mayor was thinking, but I'll need to sell it to the populace. No one is going to like it.

The Mayor said: "How about a cup of tea? Let's talk. I mean, one idea might be that you could share the place."

Lord Turnton laughed in his face. "No 'sharing'," he declared. "It's all mine. I want it back."

That seems a pretty clear position, the Mayor was thinking. No confusion there.

But who would want to hear it?

It was less than an hour later when Marilyn went round with a whistle and got everyone's attention. She herded them out of their conversations and pointed them to the right, down the slight slope and into the Conference Hall. It had been laid out with tables and chairs, Night Club style, and the low stage held nothing but a single microphone.

The 'contestants' would have to step up and speak their piece, with no visual aids.

People were slow to take their seats, preferring to stop and talk to people they knew. There was a lot of greetings, no handshakes and hugs, of course, as Covid restrictions were still in place. Still, families, including long-lost relatives, wanted to sit together, so chairs were re-arranged and people moved around to make their own arrangements.

The gabble was still going on when Marilyn stepped up to the microphone. She had to blow her whistle again.

"We all know why we're here," she stated flatly. "We have explored a lot of suggestions from various people, over the years, but here they all are again, in one space, ready to answer questions. I've got just one ask, please hear them out first."

There was grumbling at that. People sitting around the tables had clearly made up their minds long ago, and were just looking forward to being able to show their disapproval. Marilyn didn't even get a clap.

First up was a well-known local property developer. He said he was 'Salford born and bred'.

"You need a few million to do up the Manor House," he reminded them. "I don't have that to spare, but I could make the project pay if we just demolish the whole Depot area and build new houses there. That would pay for the re-furb."

He sounded quite reasonable, but there shouts of 'No houses in the park!' almost immediately. There was a caucus in the far corner, over by the French windows that opened out onto the lawn and allowed recently married couples to get pretty photos of themselves and their families amongst the flowers. No one in the corner was smiling now.

"The offer's there," the property man said, and beat a retreat. He had architect's plans under his arm.

"You just want to make money!" somebody yelled, which seemed a little unfair. He had offered to do all the work 'at cost', He wasn't looking to make a profit, he said.

Next up was a retailer. Another 'Salfordian', he said, but that was a long time ago. He lived in London now.

"I haven't forgotten my roots," he asserted. He looked to be of retirement age, but showed no sign of slowing down.

"You know my plan," he told them. "I want to turn the Manor House into a hotel, a small, boutique hotel. The ground floor will be available to the community. I'll restore the ballroom there for local events, and the West Wing can be a permanent Cafe, open to walkers, cyclists and all Salford people. I'll just need some extra bedrooms to make it a going concern - "

His plan was to use the near part of the the old Depot area and put in an annexe extension of fifty bedrooms. The bottom half of the Depot would be a car park, (which he said would be 'available' to park users).

People booed. They actually stood up and booed, trying to howl him down.

One man managed a coherent criticism. "It will mean extra traffic," he yelled. "You'll have to widen the access road and there will be cars coming in and out, day and night. It's dangerous for the kiddies! Don't you care?"

The old man protested and said he did, but by that time most people weren't listening.

Next up was a local hero, a short man with tattoos. He had 'made good' and was an example to Salford children.

He was a gangster.

"You all know me," he said, already angry. "Let me tell you a little story. I was standing back there, ready to bring you my plan and I heard somebody say that a chap has turned up, out of nowhere, and demanded the house back!"

It was a little more complicated that that, and the Mayor was willing to take to the stage and explain the Deed of Covenant, but people didn't really seem ready for a reasoned debate. The thin, threatening speaker at the mike was shouting by now, whipping up emotion. This is a guy who stood for Mayor, Mr Senate was thinking. Good Grief, he could have pipped me to the post, and what sort of state would the city be in now?

The criminal was yelling: "So what should we say to this interloper? What do you want me to say to him?"

The crowd had several suggestions, none of them pretty. They weren't interested in talking.

The talker caught the mood of the mob and was willing to give them what they wanted.

"You want me to shoot him?" he shouted. Then he said it again. "I can make the problem go away, you know I can!"

The Mayor had pushed Marilyn into a corner and was explaining the way things stood.

Marilyn nodded. She couldn't afford to alienate the Mayor. She needed his support, for her project and her future career. She stood up straight, took hold of her whistle and marched forward.

"Thank you, Mr Gauze," she told him, wheedling her way in front of the microphone.

"Al Gauze keeps his word," the bad man assured the crowd before he left, speaking over his shoulder.

Marilyn was looking to the wings, hoping for inspiration or words from the Mayor. What should she do next?

She didn't have to worry, A thin, ascetic woman, dressed all in black, came onto the stage from the other direction.

"I am Lord Turnton's lawyer," she said, taking the mic. "I can explain to you the legal position. Quiet, please."

"Where's the Lord?" someone shouted, and it became a chant. 'Show us the Lord, Show us the Lord.'

"He is outside now, talking to your very own Al Gauze," the lady said smoothly. "Everything can be explained."

She might have carried on, but there was the sound of a shot from outside the Hall. A gunshot.

The Mayor led the way as people rushed outside.

Al Gauze was on the ground, bleeding, and Lord Turnton was standing over him, looking confused.

"What happened?" Mayor Senate demanded, his voice booming, commanding.

"He's still breathing," the Lord said. "He just told me. He said, 'The Fairies did it'. That's all he said.'

Chapter Five: Folk Tale

Melia didn't hear the noise of the gunfire. She was deep in the cellars of the Manor House and no sound carried.

Good thing. The process works both ways: nobody could hear her scream, either.

The cellar was empty. No coffins. All gone.

She slumped against the wall, baffled and feeling beaten. Why had she come? What was she thinking?

In truth, it hadn't been her idea. She had met Terry in the canteen at Regional Office and he happened to mention that he'd made a Plastic Key. He tried to explain the process, but she wasn't listening. It was something to do with spraying jelly into the old lock and then, when it sets, you could bend it out and it would show the positions of the tumblers. Terry could file up a key to match them, and Bingo, there you were. He insisted on taking her down to the workshop in the cellar of Regional Office and showing her his lathe. She was a tiny bit bored, but then he handed her over a heavy, machined metal key.

"That will get you in," Terry told her. "Any time. Any weather."

But there was no reason to try it! Sure, they'd found coffins in the cellar, and sure, they were expecting them to be picked up some time, by the criminals who wanted the drugs, probably, but that job had been taken out of their hands now. It had been handed to Obs Team, the guys who kept 'observation' on people and places. Melia suspected that they'd simply hung a CCTV camera in a tree nearby, but that wasn't her problem. They would report to Gibson when the boxes were moved, and he would decide which operatives from his force would follow that up. It wasn't Melia's concern.

Still, Melia had some nagging doubts.

She remembered only too well when they found the living corpse in one of the coffins, lifted him out and rushed him to the hospital. Yes, he wasn't dead. He'd had a bottle of oxygen in there with him, like an aqualung, and presumably that was what kept him breathing when he was in the cargo hold at thirty thousand feet. Also, there was less padding in his box and more aluminium survival bags, scrunched against the sides. He himself was in a padded sleeping bag, inside an aluminium bag. It was rough, makeshift, but obviously it had worked, after a fashion.

Problem was, he wouldn't wake up. He was in a coma, lying in a hospital bed. The doctors weren't optimistic.

Melia felt she had a private stake in the situation. She had gone with the survivor in the back of the ambulance. She didn't know his name or his history, but she somehow felt involved in his life and wanted to know more.

That meant she left Terry and his friend - whatever his name was - in the cellar. They assured her, later, that they subsequently checked all the coffins, just to make sure there were no more travellers breathing and they told her there weren't any. Did they? Every box? There were a lot of boxes!

So it was that Melia hefted the key she'd been given, and that afternoon, when everyone else around seemed to leave the Manor House area and head into the Conference Suite to hear speeches, that she quietly went around the corner, down the slope, and let herself in at the side door. She was well equipped this time. She had a powerful torch.

When she shone it around in front of her, all she saw was an empty room.

Okay, maybe the bodies were moved. Maybe Obs knew about it and reported to their boss, but Captain Gibson simply hadn't told her. Or - maybe the Obs Team weren't as competent as they liked to pretend, and they'd missed the move.

In which case, Melia's Unit weren't doing their job. They'd lost the drugs!

Millions of pounds, Melia had been told. That was the estimate. How could they possibly -

There was a noise. This was soft, like a rattle, then thumps, like footsteps on stairs. Melia froze. It was impossible! The Manor House was unoccupied, everyone knew that. Unless it was the drug dealers coming back -

Melia snapped off her flash-light and pulled back into the darkness. She slowed her breathing, trying to be as quiet as she could, and listened. Nothing. It didn't happen again. But it had happened! Melia waited, then put her torch back on and moved towards where the disturbance had come from.

There was a door, a metal door.

If it was a normal door to the cellar of the house, then she would have expected there to be bolts on the far side, nothing on her side. But the reverse was true. There were heavy sliders, top and bottom. That made no sense. Why would anyone want to stop people from the house getting into the cellar - unless they were drug dealers using the cellars without the owners' permission. They'd want access from outside, which they had, and they'd want no interference from anyone upstairs. But there shouldn't be anyone upstairs! Still, there it was. Melia had heard something.

As carefully as she could, she tried the bolts. They were old and rusty, but Melia had come prepared. What would Terry have brought to this party, she asked herself? One thing was oil or oily spray, she reasoned.

She took the aerosol out of her rucksack and sprayed the bolts. Then, working them slowly back and forth, she managed to pull them back almost silently. Good, no lock, she was thinking, and she pulled the door open.

There was no light from above, but in her torchlight she could see stairs, old stone steps, leading up.

Taking her time, not rushing, she started climbing.

It was then that she smelt the coffee.

Melia came to a wooden door, and it was ajar. That wasn't deliberate, she could see, it was simply old and hanging off its hinges. Whoever the residents of the House were, maybe they were new and hadn't managed all the repairs yet.

She eased it open and found herself in a corridor. The smells were coming from her right. She padded along.

There was an open door on the left, and as she peeped around the edge of it, she saw a kitchen. Occupied.

"Don't be alarmed," she said, stepping forward.

"Who are you?" the cook squealed, lifting her peeling knife in defence.

Melia showed her I.D.

"British Security," she snapped. "It's my job to keep you safe."

"I'm perfectly safe here," the woman scoffed. "The Lord sees to that."

Melia stared, slowly clicking that she was talking about Lord Turnton, not anyone more elevated.

With a little close questioning, Melia soon established some facts; yes, the Lord have moved in, 'with his family', not telling anyone. No, no one knew about any cellars and hadn't tried exploring them. Yes, the cook was actually a 'Housekeeper' and had been with the Lord for many years. She enjoyed her work, she said. No, the Lord wasn't in.

But the main thing that struck Melia were the windows.

From outside, the windows looked boarded up, but with the panels being painted black. From inside, Melia could see the glass panels of the windows and that they were covered in that 'black-out' sheet that some people bought for their expensive cars. Those inside could see out, those outside couldn't see in.

Besides, this was obviously the back of the house. That was bound to attract less attention.

"I'll go back the way I came and let myself out," Melia told the Housekeeper. "Please make yourself available for further questioning, if that is needed." The other woman nodded. "Thank you for your co-operation."

Melia went back to the door to the cellar. Okay, I didn't ask her everything, she was thinking. But then, I didn't tell her much, either. I said nothing about the caskets. Maybe I'm hiding more than the woman preparing the Lord's dinner.

She descended the steps, anxious to get out. A thought did occur to her that the Lord 'and his family' would need a way in and out too, but she wasn't pausing to probe that question. Maybe another time.

Hurrying, she was swept by cobwebs as she ploughed through the cellar to the side door. She emerged looking a proper mess, and she didn't have to decide that for herself. She was told so.

She came around the corner, with the Conference Rooms on her left, and practically bumped into Marilyn.

"You poor dear," Marilyn burbled. "How can you go out, looking like that?"

Marilyn introduced herself, stressing her 'important' role. Melia lied. She said she was a volunteer.

"From the University?" Marilyn said. "Are you going to the Ball? Listen, Love, you can't step foot inside like that."

Melia had no idea what the tall woman was talking about. She was more concerned by the police cars still parked along the small road between the Conference Centre and the Manor House. Had something happened?

"Don't worry, I can tell you all about that," Marilyn assured her, taking her elbow. "Look, I'm going home to change. You come with me, and we will see what we can do. We're about the same size. Maybe I've got a dress - "

They walked across the lawns and crossed into the maze of terraced streets opposite. Marilyn lived off the main road in a mid-terraced house, near the College. She chattered brightly, all the way, adopting a confidential 'girlie' tone.

Melia had some idea who this person was and therefore played along, anxious to find things out. She wasn't prepared for the 'makeover' her hostess had in mind. Melia was shoved into the shower, cleaned and made up, with the sort of eyelashes and heavy mascara she hadn't worn since she was a teenager. Marilyn seemed to think it a jolly jape.

"You are my Cinders, and I am your Fairy Godmother," she told Melia, picking a flouncy dress from her wardrobe.

Marilyn seemed to be well off, judging by her range of clothes, Melia was thinking. She asked.

"I'm unemployed," Marilyn said merrily. "But I sued my last employer and got a very healthy pay-off."

She was right that the two girls were a similar height and shape. Melia had a choice of ball gown and tried for something unobtrusive. She had never liked 'Formals', Hops or Balls, but she had nothing else planned for the evening, and from Marilyn's excited recitation of the Guests, Melia thought there might be several important people there.

"Have you got me a carriage too, Godmother?" Melia asked, with a smile.

"I've got a Stretch Limo booked," she was assured.

It was true. A large car pulled up to the house in the narrow street, and the two well-dressed women piled in. There was a fridge in the back. They started with a small glass of fizzy wine. It wasn't a long journey. They had to drink quick.

The car joined the line of vehicles queuing up along the short road in front of the Manor House and down to the Conference facilities. Luckily, someone had thought to open the barrier between the trees, so the cars didn't have to reverse - they could go on and out the far gate. It turned out to be a slow process unloading the débutantes.

Marilyn, anxious to get on with it, dragged Melia out and walked her past the cars to the entrance to the Ball. Luckily, Marilyn observed, the 'unpleasantness' of the afternoon had been totally cleared away. There was no sign of Al Gauze.

Inside the massive room there was a band playing on the low stage. A real orchestra, apparently on loan from the BBC, (who were based at the bottom of the hill on Salford Quays). The area in front of the stage had been cleared of carpet, to reveal a delightful sprung dance floor. Most of the tables were set in a line along the centre, away from the walls, which allowed better access for all the waiting staff. There was plentiful food and drink. All you had to do was ask.

"Who is paying for all this?" Melia asked quietly, in a not very ladylike way.

"Every businessman who came this afternoon and tried to impress us," Marilyn said, and explained the proceedings.

"They want our support," she told Melia. "They know the Mayor won't do anything without our say-so."

There was no sign of the Mayor, but there were plenty of Councillors - uncharacteristically in dinner jackets. They looked uncomfortable in their tuxedos. They didn't wear them well.

The Lord did.

Perhaps it was the familiarity of the landed gentry, but when Lord Turnton swept in, he turned all heads. The dinner jacket was well cut and suited him. The red bow tie he was wearing was a symbol of a certain raffishness.

"I'm going to dance with him," Marilyn said, hurrying towards him like he was Prince Charming himself.

Turnton had flirted a little before, and he did so again. During the second dance, he offered actual money to Marilyn's 'Friends of the Manor House', if they would support his cause. The third dance wasn't a success: he noticed Melia.

In the next hour he bounced backwards and forwards between Marilyn and Melia as if he really couldn't decide who was the most attractive. Melia was flattered, but she was still working. She pumped him for information.

When Marilyn wasn't dancing she busied herself with 'Friends' business, locating and supporting all of her members. They were helping to organise the night, the music, the buffet for later. There was also the Raffle.

"This is a great opportunity," Marilyn told her troops. "Don't fail to drain the posh ones of all their cash."

To make sure everyone knew who she was and what were her intentions, she stopped the music at several intervals, and spoke to the attendees, stressing the need for donations. People clapped politely, but didn't seem to share her enthusiasm.

When the clock was showing midnight, Marilyn strode to the microphone and called for quiet.

"It's time to draw the Raffle," she shouted and actually blew her whistle, as she had done that afternoon.

"There are some fabulous prizes," she told them.

Melia was totally exhausted. It had been a long day and her eyelids were heavy. She wondered if all the long cars would be waiting outside to whisk their clients back home soon. She decided not to wait, but to risk it.

Leaping to her feet, she backed up against the wall and tried to leave the scene unobtrusively.

It was midnight and she fled the Ball, leaving behind a slipper in her haste.

Chapter Six: Mysteries

Deputy Director Caulfield had arrived early for work the next morning, but headed straight for the canteen.

He was restless, unhappy. He knew he would be wasting his time to go straight to his office. He couldn't settle, he needed someone to talk to, someone to share his troubles. But who? Most colleagues hated him.

Well, maybe that was a bit harsh, he reflected. They just despised him, and didn't want to be his friend.

Them Caulfield spotted Terry in the queue. When Terry had finished paying and was holding his tray, looking around for a seat, Caulfield called him over. Terry hesitated, but this was the boss. Well, Deputy Boss.

"Don't worry," Caulfield assured him. "I'm not looking to chat. This is business. I need answers."

Terry unloaded his plate of bacon and eggs from the tray, plus his mug of coffee. It was a wide table, he could keep his distance from the Deputy Director. Distance, 'Social Distance' during the pandemic. That was good for him.

Well, I can listen, he was thinking, while I eat. I don't have to invent small talk, at least. That was a blessing.

Caulfield asked, jumping right in: "Why does the Depot at Buile Hill park contain military vehicles?"

Damn, Terry was thinking. I'm going to have to talk, not just listen. My breakfast is going to get cold.

Such a pity I'm the 'Go To' guy for all the information in the Unit. He wasn't just a computer nerd, hacking into overseas bank accounts and monitoring foreign radio chatter. He was forced to hold all the history too.

Caulfield took a slurp of coffee. He didn't have a mug - too working class. He had a dainty cup, plus an entire jug. Only Caulfield could ask for and get a cafetiere. No other staff would dare to put pressure on the cooking staff like that.

"It goes back to the Second World War," Terry said, in between mouthfuls.

Caulfield sighed. Doesn't it always? Everything in Britain today was started in those Glory Days. He looked sour.

He doesn't seem interested, Terry was thinking, confused. I thought he wanted to know.

"I'm Australian," Caulfield told him. "Assume I know nothing."

Fair enough, Terry thought. That sounded believable.

"In 1940," Terry said, quoting history, "France had fallen and most people in Britain assumed the Nazis would invade."

"Ah," Caulfield said brightly, having seen the film. "The British Army was trapped at Dunkirk."

"But we got them back. Prime Minister Churchill and his 'little ships'. A third of a million men. They reported to Barracks, and within a matter of weeks were re-deployed all along the south coast. There was also the Home Guard."

"Old men with sticks?" Caulfield said witheringly, having seen the TV series.

"By this time," Terry said, cutting toast, "most of them had been issued with rifles. A lot of them were veterans of the First World War, remember. If they'd been sitting behind a hedge and seen Germans marching down the road towards them, they'd shoot. No doubt about that."

"Okay, got it. That's the Landing Grounds. That's where the action happens."

"There was a back-up plan," Terry said. "Preparations had been made. Strictly speaking, the invasion was expected at the nearest crossing point, opposite Calais, in the South East of England. Maybe Dover, or Folkstone. If the invaders broke through there, they would have found a Stop Line south of London, from the Medway to Kingston-upon-Thames."

This was all a long way away, Caulfield was thinking, in time and space. Anyway, what was a 'Stop Line'?

"A Stop Line is a series of fortifications, but discrete, so as not to alarm the population. However, if you drove up one of those roads today, coming up from Kent, you might notice the remains of pill boxes and fortified farms. It's not obvious, it wasn't meant to be, but if the British Army had been forced to retreat from the first wave of invasion, it would have found plenty of places already set up to help them mount a renewed defence. Plus, these places had stock of arms and vehicles."

"London," Caulfield said heavily. "The South East. You're telling me - "

"That was where the enemy was coming from then. If they broke through that Line, and took London, there was another Line, south of Oxford. You know Hitler had said that when he conquered England, he wanted to set up 'his' capital in Oxford? He loved the look of the place. He had a great sense of history."

That's one way of putting it, Caulfield was thinking, and poured more coffee into his cup.

Terry said: "The Lines were all north east to south west in that area, but there were other Lines, of course. There was one Line from Brixham to Bristol, to stop the Germans getting down into the South West and Cornwall."

"So?"

"So, the Lines face the other way now."

Caulfield took a deep breath. The country had been expecting an invasion in 1940, quite right, and they had taken precautions - covert and mostly secret - that would make it easier to stop the invading forces.

But this was Salford, in the North West of England - 200 miles away. Where were the invaders coming from now?

"You expecting the Scots to revolt?" he asked, sarcastically.

"Maybe they might!" Terry laughed. "No, that's a bonus. No, these days all we worry about is the Russians."

Caulfield took a deep breath. Sure, maybe thirty years ago, at the height of the Cold War, it might have seemed possible that Russian paratroops would arrive in North East Scotland and march south. But these days? The modern Russia had the same GDP as Italy. It was a much smaller bear, still growling, but not that dangerous, surely?

"We call them Heritage Arms Dumps," Terry said, finishing up, "but they're there, still. We could mount a Stop Line from Liverpool to Hull, if we had to. It might not halt a full mechanised deployment, but it would slow the nasties down!"

Terry had finished eating. He was looking around, as if eager to go and get on with some real work.

Caulfield said: "Okay, all I'm worried about is that one Depot. My neighbours are asking Salford City Council to build them some nice new houses on the site, away from the repeating floods where we are now. Is that possible?"

"Unlikely," Terry said, almost laughing. "You would need the Chief of the General Staff to OK removing the tanks."

Caulfield nodded. All right, he was thinking, I need to go further up the chain. I can do that.

"I've gotta go," Terry said. "I'm trying to find Melia. Have you seen her? She hasn't reported in and I'm worried."

Caulfield perked up at that. Melia was his favourite. He wanted to know more. If Terry was worried, that was bad.

"She was on point up near your Depot," Terry said, "observing the cellars at the Manor House."

Caulfield gasped. He knew nothing about that!

He told Terry to sit down again and tell him *that* story. He wanted to know everything.

Terry couldn't refuse a direct order. In a few short sentences, he outlined the Intel they had received about drugs coming in from Afghanistan and being stored in Buile Hill park. He made it seem almost routine.

Terry said: "So Melia was there when the boxes were delivered. What she doesn't know is that they got collected a couple of days ago, and Obs Team caught that on their CCTV cameras. Then they were able to follow the vehicle on the regular roadside cameras all the way to Irlam. They lost them down there. We don't know why they would go there."

"What's your best guess?' Caulfield said, thinking that maybe he had an idea too.

"The drug dealers want the drugs," Terry said, off-handedly, "but they'd need to get rid of the bodies first. Where can you bury a hundred dead bodies in Salford? Someone might notice. You can't just check them in to the local Crematorium. You'd need medical certificates and everything, for that. It's a mystery."

You don't need an 'official' Crematorium, Caulfield was thinking. Darn it, Terry, don't you know anything? Irlam is the place that used to have the biggest steel works in the North West. Most of the buildings were gone, of course. But they still have a couple of old furnaces, slowly rusting. Caulfield had seen them! Some previous mission -

"The caskets would be the biggest problem, of course," Terry was going on, enumerating what he saw as the issues, the problems. It was out of his comfort zone, of course. He preferred office work, with a computer screen.

Caulfield sighed inwardly, trying not to show his frustration.

Terry had said the coffins were 'luxury'. And they were Afghan? Likely they'd be made of cedar, maybe from Lebanon. You don't burn luxury, you sell it! Sure, the drug dealers would want to extract their drugs, maybe lose the bodies, but those caskets would sell for thousands of dollars in the right market - the USA!

Irlam was being developed as 'Port Salford', the new stop on the Manchester Ship Canal, nearer the sea than central Salford, and a place where container ships could access. Hire a container, put the boxes in, ship them out -

Sure, drug dealers were in a niche market, but nobody would turn down the chance to make half a million dollars, surely? It was a no-brainer. 'Luxury' caskets, stripped back to the wood. A valuable commodity.

Terry said: "But the biggest mystery is where you could get that junk processed. You'd need some serious lab equipment. It would be hard to hide. I don't see many people in Manchester having the right set-up."

Caulfield sighed inwardly, again. That was three things: the bodies, the caskets, and the unprocessed drugs. In Caulfield's head he had an answer to all three questions, and that was without investigation - just using his 'local' knowledge.

Because, of course, he knew the solution to question Number Three. He knew exactly where the drugs could be processed, turned into street-quality fare, ready for distribution down the various lines to the customers.

Oh, Terry, Terry, he was thinking. Why aren't you asking me?

Why does everybody take me for granted, he wondered? Why am I so underestimated? Why do I have to do these things alone? Why can't people include me, and use me as part of the team?

I know the answer, Terry, he was thinking.

I know exactly who would be processing the drugs right now.

And exactly where.

Chapter Seven: Faking

"That Lord Turnton is a complete fake," Marilyn said angrily, pushing her egg around the plate.

It was morning and Melia had slept fitfully. She was tired as she looked at her hostess across the table.

Melia had left the Ball in distress, but she had been right about the limo driver - he was waiting in line outside the Conference Rooms and was happy to take her back to Marilyn's house. Melia let herself in with the key that was hidden under the garden gnome at the front of the house, as she had been shown. She staggered upstairs and into bed.

When Marilyn arrived, an hour later, she joined her.

Without a word, Marilyn stripped off the party frock and lay down under the covers.

Melia was in her underwear too. She was relaxed about it, having two in one bed. It was like being in the Army again, she was thinking. Besides, she had been shown around the house earlier, and knew that while Marilyn had two bedrooms, she only had one bed. The other room was used as a storeroom, and was piled high with books, boxes and children's toys.

Marilyn got up first that day, went downstairs and started cooking. Melia woke up to the smell of something frying and the unmistakable aroma of coffee. She couldn't resist. She took her clothes off the rack in the other room, where they had been drying, and came down the stairs looking like her former self, and feeling like just a little of it.

She wanted to apologise to Marilyn for abandoning her that evening, but the girl waved that away.

"I don't blame you for leaving. That guy is a complete phoney," she said again, serving breakfast.

She lifted a mug of coffee and waved it in the direction of her laptop computer which was open, up and running, on the sideboard.

She had been doing a bit of research, it was clear, before she started cooking. It was very revealing.

"Listen," she told Melia, "I'll tell you exactly what I found out. I was talking to people last night, and they told me things. All I had to do was look up his family name, and there it was - plain as day. You wanna know the story?"

Melia said she did.

She wasn't feeling great. Melia, she had to acknowledge to herself, had maybe drunk a little too much, and certainly danced a lot more than normal. She couldn't really justify it by saying she was 'undercover', or something. What was she investigating? Were the 'Friends of the Manor House' going to teach her anything about the coffins in the cellar?

No, but the history of 'Lord Turnton' might tell her something, she realised, remembering the bizarre experience of finding the Cook and Housekeeper in the huge, seemingly empty house? Right, she needed more info on that.

Marilyn had an excellent memory for facts. She could relate the dates, and everything.

She said: "The original Turnton arrived out of nowhere and came to Salford in 1895. He was no 'Lord', but he had money and could afford to buy the Manor House. He said he had made a pile in the woollen trade in Yorkshire, but there's no trace of a family line, just him, the first guy. Then, the son, who became even richer selling uniforms to the Army, bought an even bigger mansion in North Wales, on the Great Orme. You know it? The promontory near Llandudno. You had to be rich to own land there, and no mistake. Well, it was him that gave the Manor House to the people of Salford in 1907, and moved out. It was his son that became an MP, and after a lifetime's service in Parliament was made an honorary 'Lord' during Ted Heath's government in the '70s. But - get this - it was a Life Peerage, not something that carried on. Harold Macmillan invented the 'Life

Peerage' idea, back in the 1950s when he was Prime Minister, and it's a simple reward to the cronies. You can't pass it on. Even if our friend here now - this so-called 'Lord Turnton' - is the legitimate son of the politician who got the honour, he shouldn't be using the title."

"I understand," Melia said quietly, chewing it over as she chewed her toast. "The title died with the old man."

Marilyn nodded, staring at her plate and looking miserable, as if regretting she had been taken in.

"Men," she said soberly. "I can't pick the good ones, can I?"

"Hey," Melia said, feeling a bit of solidarity. "He's a charming rogue. We all got fooled."

"I suppose," Marilyn said, thinking of the worst, "he might not even be rich. Maybe that's a lie too."

Melia nodded. There was no reason to believe anything the man said, she realised now. Which was a pity, she was thinking. Actually, she had enjoyed being whisked around the dance floor the previous evening. It was like a delicious fairy tale, for a few precious moments, and it was such a shame to puncture that balloon so abruptly.

"So, what are you planning to do today?" she asked Marilyn.

The girl looked up and smiled. "Back to the grindstone," she said cheerily.

It was clear to Melia that Marilyn's whole life revolved around Buile Hill park at the moment. Whatever else might have gone on once, perhaps when she was employed and had a job - that life was all on hold. She was the Chair of the Committee, the stalwart, the driving force behind the 'Friends' and their determined plan to rescue the Manor House.

Sure enough, when the two women had cleaned up and got out the door, they walked back down the hill and into the park. Marilyn's army had already started work and erected tents and tables for the day. There were cakes and drinks, again, all laid out, both for volunteers - who got them free - and for supporters, who were encouraged to donate.

"Today, we really get stuck into the Kitchen Garden," Marilyn announced grandly. "We've got an expert coming, somebody who works at the new RHS project at Bridgewater. We're going to get horticultural advice."

'RHS'? Royal Horticultural Society, Melia knew. And yes, they were a prestigious body, new to Salford, but moved into the area in order to work on the Old Hall at Boothstown. There was some sort of deal going on with Salford City Council, local landowners and the RHS, and it was going to involve complete restoration of the historic site and grounds.

Melia smiled. Marilyn's little project was like a tiny imitation of that grand plan. It was wonderful that the big guys were coming down to help her with her little scheme. It would be a coup for her to get that assistance. A photo opportunity.

While Marilyn assembled her followers into Work Groups, Melia saw the opportunity to slip away.

She had a project of her own on the go, and was anxious to make the next move.

The Housekeeper Melia had met in the kitchen the day before had told here that the family used 'the back door'. That's where she was headed. She was going to knock on that door - hammer, if necessary - and see who answered.

No one did.

Melia managed to evade the various people circulating at the front, and went down the path on the left - opposite the Kitchen Garden - she thought, without being noticed. Sure enough, there was a large wooden door at the back of the building, directly opposite the one at the front. But, like the one at the front, it seemed boarded up.

She looked closer.

It was then that she noticed that, although the six inch boards criss-crossing the door might once have prevented entry, all the screws on the right side of the doorway were now missing. She pulled at one of the flats, and it moved towards her. She checked the left hand side. All the battens that had once been hammered into the wooden surround and sealed the entrance had been replaced by screws. She stood back in sheer amazement. From a distance, this would still look like a sealed entrance, but now it was anything but. She hauled on the right, and the 'boarding up' swung smoothly back on its newly oiled hinges.

She took a step forward and knocked on the now exposed door.

Melia was careful to coincide her tapping with other noises coming from the front - the shouts, the laughs and the hammer of tools - so that she didn't draw attention to herself. But she tapped and tapped, then rattled the knocker. No reply.

In her head, she had concocted two plans. One was to knock on the door and see who replied, so that she could confirm who was occupying the supposedly 'empty' house. 'The Lord', but who else might be in there too?

Second, she would make contact and arrange another time to call. At that time she would invite along her colleague Terry. Then, she imagined, she could distract the inhabitants and give her nerd a chance to take a measure of the heavy, ancient lock. Using his skills and quick-setting plastic, she guessed he could take an impression and make a usable key. With that in her possession, she could come and go as she pleased, spying on the Turntons when she wanted.

That wasn't possible. There was really nobody there - unless they knew it was her and were hiding!

She stood back in frustration and gently swung the strips of wood back on their hinges, restoring the illusion of 'boarding up'. Just as well, right at that instant Marilyn came bustling around the corner.

"There you are, I've been looking for you," she said to Melia. She wasn't annoyed, just keen to get on.

"Listen, the Committee are all here now," Marilyn said. "I'm desperate for you to meet these people."

Melia acquiesced and followed her new friend round again to the front, but really, she was baffled. What did Marilyn expect Melia to do for her? Who did she think Melia was? What powers did she think Melia had?

So far, as far as Melia could see it, the help had all been one way. Wast Marilyn expecting payback now?

If Melia expected revelations, she was disappointed. The Committee were a bit of a let-down. All very nice, friendly, helpful, eager to get to know new supporters, but if they did have dark secrets they were cunningly concealed.

Melia sighed. Even while she accepted the offer of yet another cup of tea, she felt a sinking feeling. These aren't my sort of people, she was thinking sadly. Nobody is that interesting. Nobody else seems to be a spy or a Secret Agent.

The only one who looked as though they might have something about them was a young woman called Suze. Marilyn introduced her as 'Snooze', as though that was somewhat significant, but she didn't explain further.

Suze had a bit of energy about her, Melia noted. She seemed a little more animated than the rest. In fact, a bit on edge, as if she was expecting something bad to happen, all the time. She was looking around, nervously.

Then it did.

"Who invited him?" she spluttered, pointing at a tall man over by the raised beds. He had long, black hair and a scraggly beard, and was wearing big boots and thick sweaters, as if he really was a professional gardener.

She rushed towards him.

"Is this your horticultural expert?" Melia asked Marilyn, thinking of the RHS and the visitor she'd been told about.

"He would like to think so!" Marilyn scoffed. "No, that's Dirk from the project down the hill. He's been working on bringing the old bowling green down there back into use as small allotment plots. He's got a set of raised beds, and Suze had one, but gave it up. They fell out. She really doesn't like him anymore."

Melia stared - and listened. There were raised voices. In fact, Suze was howling at Dirk. Melia had rarely seen such animosity. Like a moth to a flame, she was drawn nearer, but the conversation made no sense.

"I wanted your help," Suze shouted, "and you turned me away. You know I had problems!"

The man Dirk replied, as calmly as he could: "I referred you to the appropriate Services - "

"That's not what you're supposed to do!" Suze told him.

He didn't seem to agree.

Melia turned to Marilyn again, and said, as quietly as she could: "Do you know what's going on?"

Apparently, it wasn't quiet enough. Suze heard her comment, and in fury rounded on Melia instead. A new victim.

"Nobody knows!" Suze yelled. "Or understands Nobody listens. You just can't hear what I'm saying!"

That was a little ironic, Melia was thinking. The way this woman has shouting, people could have heard her all the way to Liverpool. Okay, she was clearly distressed, but Melia wasn't the right person to target. Nor was Dirk.

Melia was surprised, taken aback, that emotions could run so high in a small-scale, local growing project.

Maybe I've underestimated these people, she was thinking.

I need to know more.

Chapter Eight: Folk Tale

The Woodcutter and his wife went out of their cottage to look for their lost children.

"I have no money to give," the man said, "but I will beg and plead, with everything I am."

His wife looked at him reproachfully. She knew he had not told her the whole story of what happened to their children and where they went. She did know he came back from the woods with no children and no money.

She hated him for that.

The pair started in the forest at the top of Old Buile Hill, but they found nothing, no one and no clues. They walked down the path at the back of the forest, almost to the road, and then saw the elves coming out of the cistern.

They drew closer.

The streams from the hill drained into a round pond, walled and overgrown. People called it a cistern and ducks made it home. As they approached, the Woodcutter and his wife saw that there was an iron door in the back wall and it was open. Little people were coming through, climbing the steps and forming a procession, going on down towards the gate of the park.

It was easy to think they were elves: they were dressed in bright green jackets and wore strange little hats.

The Woodcutter wanted to stop one and ask them if they knew his children, but he was interrupted.

He wife was screaming.

She was at the back of the line and she had recognised her children in the procession, but they didn't know her.

The Magus wasn't far behind. He had paused to close the metal door, but now he was at the top of the steps.

"My children! My children!" the distraught woman was wailing, tearing her hair.

The Magus stepped up to his full height and glared down at her, swirling his cloak around him.

"They are my children now," he told her, without pity.

"I beg you," the Woodcutter said, "please release them. We want them home with us."

The Magus said: "That is never going to happen. They are part of the elf family now. Today we go to church, as usual. It is all part of their new life with me. Look at them - do they seem unhappy? They are well dressed and well fed."

"I can't guarantee to do that for them," the woman admitted, "but I bore them. I need to raise them."

The magic man scoffed. "I can do a better job," he told her.

"In the name of the Lord," the Woodcutter shouted, "I plead with you to let them go!"

The Magus was about to continue his journey, but he stopped in his tracks. His face went suddenly blank.

"Halt!" he yelled at the little people. "Cease your perambulation. Await my command."

The elves stood stock still, even the ones nearest the gate. They didn't look round, but seemed paused, at least.

The woman said: "You're going to reconsider?"

The Magus stared at her. "Your husband has used the magic word. I must obey his command."

"So you will let them go?"

"I grant you Three Wishes," the Magus said to the Woodcutter. "Use them well."

The Woodcutter paused. He looked at his wife. Tears were streaming down her cheeks. He knew what she wanted.

"I wish," he said grandly, "that our two children should return with us, to live in our little cottage in the woods."

The Magus leant down from his great height, brushed his long black hair out of his face, and whispered to the boy and the girl. He seemed to be chanting something at them, as if making or unmaking a spell.

The two children looked up, and for the first time there was recognition in their eyes.

They rushed to their mother and embraced her. Without pausing, she turned them round and hurried them all off back to their little house. She didn't pause for gratitude, afraid that whatever boon had been granted might be withdrawn.

The Magus seemed to have lost interest in the proceedings. He turned back to his line of little people in their smart uniforms and set them in motion again. The Woodcutter, stunned by the turn of events, watched speechless as the procession crossed the road and went into the grounds opposite.

That's the School, he was thinking. The local Primary School. Is that where they hold their 'church' on a Sunday like today? But it was afternoon. Why didn't they worship in the morning? It was most unusual.

Then, turning around, he set off up the path, back to the family home.

The idyll did not last long.

The Woodcutter's wife dressed the children in some of the clothes they had left behind, and then reminded them of their old routine. They seemed reluctant to go to school, but she forgave them that, and kept them at home for the first day, so they could re-orientate themselves and remember what their parents were like.

The two young people seemed a little lost in their old world, and had to be told where everything was - the bathroom, the toothbrushes, their own bedroom. Their mother began to feel as though she hadn't recovered her previous children, but had somehow been given a new boy and girl, sent to her so that she could adopt them.

Still, in the evening, relaxing in front of their blazing log fire, she could look at their little faces as they lay on the huge rug and she could remember former times, when they were happy as one family. Those times would come again, she was thinking. The poor children are unsettled, confused. She will help them remember and all would be well.

The next morning, when she awoke, the children were gone, as was most of the family's possessions.

The wife's loud wailing brought the Woodcutter from his bed. He looked around, not sure what was happening.

"They have take everything!" he wife informed him. "The little thieves! Who has made them like this?"

There was only one possible answer, and that was the man who had been their substitute parent and Guardian.

The Woodcutter picked up his axe, intending to go looking for the Magus. His wife came in and stopped him.

"I've found this card in the children's bed. Perhaps it's a way to contact him," she said.

The card read 'Uncle Magnus, Children's Entertainer', and there were lots of flowers around the words.

The wife dialled from her phone and the Magus answered. He sounded quite chipper, on speaker-phone.

"Well, of course they stole from you," he said gleefully. "They've been trained."

"Then it's time for my Second Wish," the Woodcutter said, seizing the phone. "You've trained the children to steal? Fine. Then let them live with us and steal from other people. Anything they find they can give to you - I don't want it. I just wish to see my children living under my roof. You are driving my good wife to illness, and it must stop."

He was waving the axe, as though the Magus would be able to see the threat. It certainly drove the magic man to silence. There was a pause from him. Meanwhile, the husband and wife could here children happily playing.

"You've given me a challenge," the Magus said at last. "The idea they could steal, but not from you - Well, it's a fresh concept, I do declare. Still, it could be profitable, as you intimate. You want me to go ahead with it? You're sure?"

The couple loudly declared they were certain, and within hours the children came back through the door.

This time, they were a lot more loving to their parents, and happy to join them for lunch and dinner. The only disconcerting element is that they insisted on going out at night, after dark, and returning with sacks of loot, before tumbling into bed at midnight. It made them even more ill prepared to go to school, as they slept in the next morning and couldn't be stirred.

"They are still only old enough for the Primary School," the wife said to the Woodcutter, "but when they are grown, and ready for the Higher School, then we will re-visit our decision and see if we need to amend our decision."

Unfortunately, Life intervened, long before that day.

It was in the form of uniformed constables knocking on the Woodcutter's wooden door. The weren't amused.

"We have had all kinds of reports of the activities of your children," one said. "Don't try and deny it."

"We have a Warrant to search your premises," the other said, and that was the end of that. The children's room was so stuffed with stolen household goods - with no explanation - that they were whisked into a police car in no time and taken down to the Police Station. The adults had to make their own way there. The Woodcutter's wife was in tears. Again.

They had to wait all night before they were allowed to see the children again.

"We have been contacted," the police Sergeant at the desk said, as if that explained everything. "You can take them home now, but you will have to report back on this date - " and he handed them a piece of paper.

It was dawn. Within the hour, the Woodcutter was back at the top of old Buile Hill, hunting for the Magus.

He found the magic man walking up and down, outside the Manor House. Up and down, as if on patrol.

"I have one more Wish," the Woodcutter told him angrily. He had no weapon, but his blood was up.

"Better make it good this time," the Magus advised him. "You have a habit of choosing wrong."

The Woodcutter felt deflated. It was true. He had been given all the freedom there was. He could have chosen anything, and he made a mistake - two mistakes - in choosing a path that only led to disaster, for both him and his loved ones.

Perhaps he simply wasn't up to it. The choosing was beyond him, he was thinking. It made him feel inadequate.

"I wish for help," he declared. "Heaven send me an Advisor, someone who can break this awful chain of events."

Now, as it happened, the Lord of the Manor came riding past at that very moment.

Lord Turnton heard the Woodcutter's cries, and pulled his pretty white stallion to a halt. He looked down from his seat, then climbed gingerly down to the ground. Holding the reins, he asked for more details of the dilemma.

The Magus seemed nervous about talking to a real-life Lord, and insisted on moving aside, so that the Woodcutter would not hear the details of their conversation. The Woodcutter stared. Was there money involved? He had none, he was sure of that. Would the Lord be prepared to put up the funds to buy the children back?

At last, after what seemed like an age, the Lord came over to the Woodcutter, smiling.

Where was the Magus? He seemed to be stealing away, heading down the hill. Where was he going?

"I have persuaded the Wizard to call at your house now, right now," the Lord said, "and lift the veil that covers your children's eyes. He has been hypnotising them, did you know that? He has been using low tricks and deceit. He seemed strangely proud of his skills, but I have managed to persuade him to reverse the process."

The Woodcutter fell to his knees. "My Lord," he said, choking, "I have no way to repay you!"

"Maybe not now," the Lord agreed. "But I'm confident in saying that there will come a time when I will ask a favour of you, and at that time, it would be churlish of you to refuse me, would it not? Please consider before you answer."

The Woodcutter nodded and nodded, but his head was whirling and he had not really heard what the man with the horse had said. He was just so grateful - How had the Lord done it? Blackmail? Threats?

"I can never thank you enough for what you've done," the Woodcutter repeated. "Lord, what can I do for you?"

"I will tell you soon enough," the Lord said, turning around and getting back into the saddle.

He was laughing as he walked his horse sedately away.

"Some day soon, Woodcutter," he shouted. "We will meet again, you and I."

Chapter Nine: Explanations

The next time Melia went up to Buile Hill she was surprised to bump into Dirk Forrest.

She didn't really know what she was expecting that day, but the sun was shining and there was no sign of the regular Salford showers. She just wondered what the Manor House would look like when there was no one there, no crowds of eager supporters, no furious activities. She came down the path from the main road and was surprised to see Dirk coming up the other way, walking along beside the high hedge. He didn't seem to notice her when he jumped the fence and went into the deserted Depot.

Melia was intrigued. What was he doing? Was he looking for something? Somebody?

She saw where he had entered. There was a sort of electrical junction box against the wall. Climbing onto that, it was a short haul up onto the top of the fence, and a light drop down the other side. Maybe this was how the vandals get in, she was thinking, the ones that have wrecked the brick buildings, throwing off the tiles and setting fires.

Melia looked around. The tall figure of Dirk was in the distance, going down the slope towards the old wooden greenhouses, set against the far railings. Now what was that about, she wondered?

When she caught up with him, he told her.

Dirk Forrest seemed unembarrassed to have been caught trespassing. He greeted Melia with a smile and offered to 'show her round'. But this wasn't part of his part of the park, surely, she said. Your project is further downhill?

"Look at these structures," he said eagerly. "The glass is gone but the wood frames are completely intact."

"There's plants growing out of them there!" she protested. It was a wild area, becoming overgrown.

"We just need a bit of money," he said. "We could raise a geodesic dome over the lot, and that would give us time to work on restoring the greenhouses. No rain, no rot. The weeds would soon be replaced by useful plants."

She stared at him. He had some wild ideas, she was thinking, but he was full of enthusiasm and willing to share his dreams with whoever is passing by. Maybe he's hoping I can help him, she thought? But who does he think I am?

"I'm a volunteer with Marilyn - " she started, trying to build a cover story.

He cut her off. "I used to be involved with the Manor House group too, but they didn't like my approach," he explained. "They constantly wanted to cut corners. They organised a big day of activities in Spring and let dozens of people into the Kitchen Garden with no masks, no distancing. We'd just come out of Lock-down, for Goodness' sake. Covid is still a danger for everyone, young and old. They're irresponsible!"

Melia nodded. She could imagine Marilyn cutting corners and ignoring 'Guidelines' in her desire to get on, get things done. But was Dirk any different? He had big plans too. Would he stick to the Rules to make things happen?

"I love this place," he told Melia. "It looks like a ruin, right? And the roofs have gone, there and there, and there's nothing showing but the timber frames. Still, check it out. The buildings are still watertight at ground level."

Melia looked, as suggested. He was right! That was odd she was thinking. The 'vandals' weren't doing a very good job of wrecking! Was it just meant to look beyond repair, so people would give up and leave the place alone?

Dirk said: "My dream has always been to have a Garden Centre in here. We'd need some roofs, certainly, but you could throw tarpaulins over some of sheds with missing tiles, then install see-through roofs actually arching between the buildings - either plastic or glass - and that would be your growing areas for seedlings, and display areas for Sales."

Melia nodded. Yes, she could see that.

He said: "My project is down the hill and we just haven't got enough space for glasshouses and display areas. But if we had this site as well - " He stared, like a man seeing a distant vision. "It would all be viable, self-sustaining."

"I think I need to see your other site," she told him, angling for an invitation.

"Certainly," he said. "My pleasure. Let's get out of here."

On the way up the slope to the climbing wall, Dirk pointed out the various buildings.

It had been more than a 'Council Depot'. That was just the big brick buildings where the vehicles were stored. Opposite that, was a full, detached house, that was used as Offices. Back near the historic wood glasshouses, there were a number of smaller aluminium greenhouses, that had been used for growing, he assured her. For many years it had been a place where teenagers who couldn't go to regular school could be offered some work experience and training.

It was a large area, she realised, and 'multi-purpose'. A lot of groups and organisations must have lost out when it was closed. Dirk listened when she said that, and agreed. He could offer similar services, he said, when the time came.

Melia was fit and agile, but she was grateful for a push from Dirk to get up on top of the wall. A little too intimate, she wondered? Oh well, he was a good-looking man. A little flirting was always welcome. She enjoyed his company.

He led her to the left of the Depot, the opposite side to the Manor House. It was all woods there, dark and mysterious, but he seemed to know the way. They moved steadily downhill, till they came out on a path going east-west.

"This is the old boundary," he told her, "between Seedley Park and Buile Hill. It's all one now."

Melia nodded. Marilyn had told her a little of the history, when they were both at Marilyn's house, eating and spending time together. The place we now call 'Buile Hill', the girl had said to Melia, is actually an amalgamation of three separate estates, that the Council had acquired and brought together. That was why it was the biggest park in Salford now.

Dirk stopped, looking left and right. Melia paused too, ready for more history.

"In front of us are green railings, going left and right," Dirk said, showing off his little empire. "Everything within the railings is what I'm interested in, even though that bowling green you can see on the right is mostly used by the Croquet Club, and the Pavilion you can see in front of you, in the distance, is home to The Friends of Buile Hill."

Melia smiled. Everywhere has got 'Friends', she was thinking. Everywhere here. Maybe we all need 'Friends', she wondered.

She asked: "But I thought you did planting. Growing stuff. That's what people say."

Dirk agreed. "The trees you can see on the left here conceal the other bowling green that used to be there. Now, it's all be been converted into allotment plots, small areas that individuals can work for themselves and common areas that other people can share - people like the 'Incredible Edible' group. They have five little patches for themselves."

They kept moving downhill, keeping to the left of the railings. On their far left, leading away from the path, there was a large area of lawn, intersected by a small wooded area, a copse, and other paths, going in all directions.

"They do say," Dirk said wistfully, "that when this area was first opened as a park, back in Edwardian days, that there was a lake here, ducks, seats and a bandstand. It couldn't be maintained. It all got cleared away."

They had to walk to the far end of the green railings, then up a slight rise to a gate, a padlocked gate.

"We don't open every day of the week," Dirk explained. "But I've got keys. I'll show you around and then we can have a cup of tea in the Pavilion. Okay, turn right and let's see the growing area."

There were trees on the right, which is why that part of the site wasn't visible from the path. Melia realised, almost at once, that this half of the whole thing must have once been a bowling green, as Dirk said. It was square, with bushes on all sides. The 'plots' were there, as he described, and mostly raised beds, which would be great for those who couldn't bend.

Dirk took Melia up one side and they walked through the trees against the railings - a Woodland Walk - then came back across a brook, and alongside a pond. Melia was impressed. It was a lot, in a seemingly small space.

"How long has this been here?" Melia marvelled.

Dirk smiled. "Two years to get to this, but there was some earlier work done, about ten years ago." He told her the long story.

He had been employed way back then, nearly a decade before, to make the first moves in helping to convert the abandoned bowling green into a growing area. It had been paid for and managed by a local mental health charity, 'Going Places', as a way of helping people recovering from mental illness, by providing them with an open air space they could work on and enjoy. Also, it was sociable. They could meet other people, similar to themselves.

It didn't last. The charity ran out of money, and the space was abandoned. Dirk went off to do another job, this time in Manchester, but two years ago, they ran out of money to pay him and he suddenly found himself at a loose end. Coming out for a walk, he saw the Seedley site and it gave him an idea to come back and work there again. This time for free.

"That sounds wonderful," Melia said. "All for nothing?"

"I had some redundancy money," Dirk laughed, "and when I started coming here regularly, the word spread and some of the old users turned up. That was great for a while, them coming back and claiming their old plots, but then - "

Melia waited. Yes? There were problems?

Dirk's mood had changed. His brow furrowed and he looked troubled and upset.

"You've met Suze, haven't you?" he asked. Melia nodded. "It's all a misunderstanding, really. When the place was first opened, it was there for people with mental health challenges and it had staff to support them. Suze saw me organising things and assumed I had been put there to provide therapy, or something. She kept saying she 'needed support'. I tried to divert her to the regular Services, but she kept saying, 'It's your job! You should help me.' I really didn't know what else to do - "

"Nobody was paying you!" Melia gasped. "Have you got any qualifications in that area?"

Dirk took a breath. "Actually, I have, but it's only something I've acquired in the last few years. I haven't had much experience in counselling yet, and I certainly couldn't take on anyone here as a client, not without more training."

No, Melia was thinking. If someone like Dirk started offering treatment, well, that could end badly.

Dirk shook himself, like a dog throwing off water.

"Time for tea," he said, moving on from bad memories. "Let's get in to the Pavilion. I'll put the kettle on."

As they walked up to the Pavilion, a thought occurred to Melia, and she put a hand on his elbow.

"This bit looks well cared for," she said, remembering the Depot. Do you ever get vandals here?"

Dirk smiled "We get kids coming over the fencing," he said easily. "But I talk to them. I tell them they're welcome as long as they don't damage anything. They seem to respect that. I'm certainly not going to act as Security Guard, paid or not!"

Melia was impressed. This man seemed to have a caring and respectful attitude. She'd begun to like him, a lot.

Suddenly, there were a number of loud bangs, coming from the direction of the Depot.

"Bonfire Week," Dirk said ruefully. "The kids are always setting off fireworks this time of year."

Melia didn't want to disagree with the man, but she clearly had more experience with firearms than he had.

That was the sound of small arms fire, she was thinking. Maybe the Depot has Guards, even if there were none here.

But who were they shooting at? And who would they be allowed to shoot?

Chapter Ten: Betrayals

Mr Caulfield was out on the streets, visiting his neighbours.

The first door he happened to knock on belonged to the local Flood Warden.

"The Council's let us down," she said, on her doorstep, then, remembering her manners, she invited him in.

They sat down on her leather couch, sipped tea in mugs, and she let the Council have it, both barrels.

"They promised," she stormed, "that when the Flood Basin was built on the old racecourse, that it would drain away excess water when the river stared to rise. Get it? No more floods! Has it happened? Has it Buxton!"

Caulfield nodded, not following the words, but picking up the gist. She was disappointed the flood prevention plan wasn't working. That was odd, he agreed. He'd seen the Basin, it was on the opposite side of the river to his house, a huge bowl in the bend of the river, with access gates on both sides. When the water level was high, the gates would open and water would rush in from the upriver side. When levels started down, water could be released on the downriver side.

It was a wetland, now, with lots of wading birds, unique flowers and fauna. A good place to walk your dog.

Caulfield didn't own a dog, but he could appreciate the joy such an animal might bring.

The woman seemed remarkably cynical, he was thinking, but was that because she knew too much?

"Before the basin was built," she told him, "the only way to control water levels was to open the sluices at Mode Wheel locks. But that would have threatened flooding further downstream - Warrington, maybe, or Cheshire. You see?"

The Deputy Director was not totally understanding what seemed like a political problem, or perhaps one of socio-economic status. But he did get that this woman thought she'd been let down.

Maybe because she had bought her own house?

The 'Right to Buy' legislation that Mrs Thatcher had passed in the 1980's had made a creeping change to the area. Before then, Strike Island had been all Council Houses, owned and managed by the Local Authority. Then, as individuals bought their properties, one at a time, it had gradually changed the whole feel of the place. There was a new mood.

You could tell the 'bought' houses, because they were the ones that were painted and had tidy gardens. The new owners took a pride in their properties, and promptly changed the political party they voted for - as intended.

These house-proud voters didn't support the Labour Party in Salford anymore, but strangely, their new-found freedom made them more demanding of Council services. They had become acutely aware of their 'rights'. Like this woman here: it was her house, and she demanded it be protected. She wanted the Council to guarantee it wouldn't be flooded.

Caulfield had a question. He tried to frame it in an unthreatening manner.

"Does everyone support your campaign?" he asked gently.

"Everyone in my street!" she said at once. "I can't speak for the criminals on the far side. Ask Fran."

Ah, that was what the Deputy Director wanted to know. He was looking for the 'criminals'. Exactly.

The woman 'Fran' that had been suggested, lived at the far end of the street, away from the river, but more into the middle of the estate. Yes, she might have more information on the wrong 'uns, then, the bad guys.

Caulfield knocked on her door and again, was welcomed in. Fran seemed eager to talk.

The story that Mr Caulfield cobbled together was that he was 'new to the area', and that seemed enough to open the flood-gates. If he'd been a reporter, or someone from Law Enforcement, the residents might have been more circumspect, but as a newcomer to the patch, they were keen to warn him of the dangers.

"'Neighbourhood Watch," Fran declared, handing the man an obligatory cup of tea. "That's me, me and Dottie on the road behind. Well, a few more, and we get out sometimes at night, and there's men there then. They don't like the idea of their wives walking the streets with flash-lights. But there's precious few of us, I can tell you."

Tell me, Caulfield urged. He wanted to know everything.

"They start young," she told him. "It's a bit of vandalism, and the parents say, 'Oh, they're just growing up, finding their feet'. But they don't understand - the kids who start with a bit of graffiti and brick throwing, move on to shoplifting, and by the time they're teenagers it's cars. Either they break in and steal the radio, or they take the whole car. Either way."

Caulfield nodded, glad of the analysis. Criminality ran in families, then?

"It certainly does," she said. "On the next corner there's the Receivers. You know the type? Kids arrive on their doorsteps with mobile phones and radios, and the woman buys them cheap, no questions asked. Where does it all come from? Who cares! She just sells it on, making a profit, but not thinking: my back door gets broken, and the little louts are in here, grabbing what they can? It ends up in her lounge. She doesn't care. It's all just easy money."

"What about the Criminal Code?" he asked. "I've lived in Hong Kong for a while. There, there was an understanding that you don't rob off your neighbours. You're a community. You stick together. You're all in the same boat."

Fran laughed outright, amazed at the man's naiveté.

"But we're not!" she said scornfully. "We might all be facing the same storms, but we're in different little ships. I've bought my own house, that's one group of people. Then there are the people who've been renting for years, and their whole family is nearby. Sure, they're respectable, hard working. No, the ones we have to fear are the new arrivals - no offence - but if the Council has re-housed them here, then they've probably been chucked out from where they were before, for bad behaviour, or not paying the rent. Why do we have to get given the dregs? What have we done?"

Ah, but it's not even 'the Council' anymore, is it, he was thinking? Those municipal houses were given away to independent Housing Associations by the Coalition government, in the last decade. You can't blame the existing Council!

Of course, that was Fran's problem. She wanted someone to blame. It had to be the Council's fault!

Caulfield got up to leave, but he needed a bit more information, something definite.

"It can't be that bad, surely," he suggested. "Is it just the case of a few rotten apples?"

"Oh, there's plenty of those," she said, and went to the window. "See that house opposite, two along? That's old Jim, and he says that the place behind is a drugs den. They're growing cannabis in the attic. Dreadful smell, all day."

This is more like it, Caulfield was thinking. This is exactly what I need.

Fran stopped him on her doorstep, determined to not let him get away with the wrong idea. Crime *was* rife.

"The thing I don't understand is the bus stops," she said angrily. "Look out for them. You go out in the morning, and the bus shelter has been attacked, the glass smashed. Why? What good does that do anybody? Who are you hurting?"

Caulfield nodded. The people who actually needed a bus were the young, the old and the infirm. People without cars were already second-class citizens. If they had to walk through broken glass to even get into town -

"They don't think," he said, trying to imagine what it would be like to be a teenager living around here now.

"It's unforgivable," Fran declared flatly, and let him go.

Caulfield was a little taken aback by her vehemence, but then, he was new. He didn't know what real residents felt.

He walked up to the corner, following the directions he had been given, went around the corner and down the road.

It didn't take a detective to tell which one was the cannabis house. He could smell it from the top of the street, plus the fact that the windows were blacked out, and yet there were lights on, clearly, shining through, around the edges. Strong lights, strong smell? It was a cannabis farm. He was going to enjoy this.

He knocked on the door. There was scuffling behind it, as though people weren't expecting visitors and decided to tidy up before they opened the door. Then, when there was an answer, it was a young man, opening just a slit.

"Waddya want?" he asked, clearly baffled by the podgy man in the smart suit. It was clearly better than he could afford.

"I'm here on business," Caulfield said brightly. "Is the boss man in? The head honcho?"

"You want some weed?"

"I was hoping for something a little stronger."

The kid looked at him. The poor thing was confused. This man - he wasn't a Policeman?

"You p'lice?" he asked, just to check.

"Sure, I'm in the Intelligence Unit," Caulfield said. "This won't concern you."

The youngster stepped away, but left the door slightly open. There was someone behind him, it seemed.

Now that man came forward. There were a lot of tattoos, clearly seen, since he was only wearing a t-shirt and shorts.

It must be warm in there, Caulfield was thinking. The man was sweating profusely.

"I was told you might be able to help me," Caulfield said, making it up. He confidently felt superior to this rabble, anyway. He wasn't going to have any trouble, he was thinking. I will overwhelm them with my charm.

"Who are you? I've never seen you before," the man told him.

"I've just moved in to the area," he was told. "Truth is, I'm an accountant, but I believe we are in the same business."

"So you say?" the man said sceptically. "And what do you want from me?"

"I want to speak to the people who are processing the drugs from the Manor House coffins," Caulfield said.

The other man looked as if he had been slapped in the face. He was quite nonplussed.

"That's nothing to do with us," he said, at last, stammering. "You want to speak with that lot? Okay, your funeral. Go to the end of the street, turn right, second right. Colombia Street, number 94. Don't say I sent you."

"My lips are sealed," Caulfield said with a smile, glad he had found out some more information.

The man grimaced, then chuckled. "You get on the wrong side of those boys, and your lips will be sealed, forever."

Talks tough, Caulfield was thinking, not impressed. Small scale cannabis farm? Not really international criminals!

But they knew the people he was looking for. The Big Boys. Ironically, this guy was giving him the address, as if to say, 'Go ahead, walk into the Lion's Den. See what happens!' Caulfield was more confident than he should have been, but still -

The Deputy Director, temporarily off-duty, followed the instructions and found the house in question.

There was no smell this time, and they had made an effort to disguise the current use by having the front curtains open to show a typical Living Room, with television and sofas. The rest of the house will be the factory, Caulfield guessed.

He knocked boldly on the door and waited politely for an adequate reply.

A man in a suit answered, looked Caulfield up and down, He did seem strangely relaxed.

"You calling for money?" the man said blandly.

Caulfield thought about it. 'Protection'? Is that what he expected?

"I've just moved in," Caulfield said again. "Peru Street. The fact is I'm an accountant. I represent some very important people. I'm thinking they might be extremely interested in your product, if you're looking for a new outlet."

The man considered that, as if it was a perfectly ordinary thing to ask, in daily business.

Instead of giving an answer directly, he said: "Peru Street? That's the new houses, isn't it? You're on the flood plain. They didn't tell you that when you purchased. You're feeling aggrieved and want the Mayor to solve your problem. There's a suggestion he could arrange to build you some houses in Buile Hill park, using the land that used to be the Council Depot. But the Mayor has already given support to 'The Friends of the Manor House' group, and they want the Depot. Also, he's got his 'In Tray' full of complaints about poor quality build and inflammable cladding on high-rise flats. Tell me, which crisis is he going to attend to first, do you think?"

Caulfield said: "I don't think he knows about the coffins in the cellars of the Manor House and he doesn't realise you're bringing in pre-processed drugs. By the time he finds that out - "

"By that time," the man said. "We will have moved on and arranged another route. It's just a short term need, what with the Afghan situation being what it is. Another couple of weeks and there will be a new store. Don't worry."

"Oh, I'm not worried - "

"It's all about money," the man told him. "If you - or whoever you're involved with - has some to offer, then I'm listening. Right now, I have quite a lot, actually. Money to 'launder', you might say. You want to sell me your house? I'll buy it, and give you a good price - for a new house prone to flooding. You won't get anyone else to give you cash."

"You're in the property business?" Caulfield couldn't help but ask. This seemed so ludicrous! What about the drugs?

"I own most of this street," he was told. "Starting ten years ago, I started encouraging the Council House tenants to exercise their Right to Buy. The house might be valued at a hundred thousand, say, and the Council would have to give them a healthy discount, say forty per cent. So, we'd give the residents the sixty grand to buy the house, then give them the other forty for their trouble, plus the opportunity to carry on living there, rent free. It was an offer they couldn't refuse. We couldn't make them move straight away, because the 'Right to Buy' rules said they had to stay living there for a minimum of five years. So we waited. After five years we told them to go, and gave them five thousand expenses. So they did. By that time they'd spend the 40k anyway, and have to go back to renting, but somewhere else."

"This is all very fascinating - "

"I'm only telling you this because you're an accountant," the man said. "I thought you might be interested."

Caulfield felt himself being boxed into a corner. He knew he was going to have to find a way out of it.

The man said: "So, you coming in? We going to do some business here today?"

Caulfield stirred himself, then reached into his pocket and pulled out a roll of bills.

"No, I tell you what we're going to do," he said to the man. "I'm going to give you fifty pounds now. You're going to go into your lab and cut me a slice of product, then slip it into a small plastic bag. I'll take it away now and have my boys test it. If they're all happy, I'll come back here and spend two hundred thousand with you, half in crypto currency."

The man grunted, as if the plan seemed reasonable.

"Wait here," he said, going back inside but leaving the door open, in a trusting kind of way.

Caulfield was livid. Why would he trust me, he was thinking? Why should I trust him? Not only does he wreck people's lives by hooking them into a lifetime habit of dangerous drugs, but he also takes their houses off them!

Caulfield felt like crying.

Losing your house? It was just what happened to his father, back in Australia.

Chapter Eleven: The Emperor

Later that day, Melia came across Lord Turnton in the park, having his car taken away.

She had decided to take time to explore more of Buile Hill, so after leaving Dirk's growing area, she walked down the path along the fence. It took her down to the sump, the round, brick-lined pond near the far gate, but she had no idea it was in any way significant. She rounded the corner then, and headed back uphill with the old Pitch and Putt area on her left. The Conference Rooms came into view, on her right, with the Manor House beyond. But on her left was another tree-lined roadway, leading up to a middle gate. This is where she found the Lord, under the trees.

He made excuses.

"There's something wrong with the suspension," he said grandly, as though the low loader that was taking the car away was from some local garage, and his vehicle was heading for repair.

That might have been believable, except for the fact that the Range Rover towing the trailer actually had the words 'Ron's Repo's' painted on the side. The operative, big and in oil stained overalls, did look like a 'Ron', Melia thought.

"It's the Repo man," she told Turnton. "You haven't been keeping up your payments and he's taking the car away."

He nodded, shame-faced, but he wouldn't admit it out loud. He still had some pride left.

Melia gazed at the Lord in wonder. How are the mighty fallen, she was thinking in wonder.

The last time she'd seen him, at the Ball, she had considered him a Prince. What had gone so wrong, so suddenly?

She stayed with him, but his side, while the other man did his duty, revved up his engine and drove himself, the trailer and the kidnapped car slowly out of the park.

It was only then that Melia noticed the horse, amongst the trees. He was tied to a stake in the ground, and was happily grazing, but not for long. As Lord Turnton's car disappeared out of his life, another Land Rover came into view, towing a horse box.

It drove slowly towards them, then parked on the grass verge.

"Not the horse too!" Melia gasped. "They're not taking that!"

Turnton hung his head in shame, while another Repo Man walked over and untied the horse from its tether, then led the animal on the short rope towards the horse box. The man opened the back and led the magnificent horse inside.

"Sign!" the man told the Lord, after, producing a form on a clipboard. Thoughtfully, he provided a pen.

"This is only temporary," Turnton burbled as he put his signature at the bottom of the form and signed his horse away.

Melia still didn't move. She had never witnessed such disgrace and really, didn't know what else to do.

She felt a little solidarity with the man. We've all fallen on hard times sometime, she was thinking. Even me.

Lord Turnton seemed reluctant to leave the scene, but soon there was only the tracks of the horse box on the grass as evidence of anything. The man had even taken the stake out of the ground.

Perhaps it was valuable, Melia was thinking.

Shaking himself, Turnton turned to his companion and said: "You must come in and join me for coffee."

'Come in'? Melia was wondering. Into the Manor House? Why yes, she wanted to see inside.

That had been one of her plans. Now she wouldn't need to break in, so that was a bonus, she was thinking.

The pair walked up the slight slope in silence, then around the back of the building, without a word.

Turnton produced a large metal key from his pocket. He pulled on the boards and they swung open, then he put the key in the old lock and it turned easily, like it had been oiled. He opened the door and ushered Melia in.

She dallied in the lobby while the man pulled the boards together behind them, then locked the door, with grace. He put the key on an old-fashioned table on one side. When he said he would start the coffee and headed for the kitchen, Melia said something about 'the toilet' and watched him go. Then she pulled out her phone and photographed the key.

Terry could make a copy from these pictures, she was thinking, satisfied.

She didn't actually look for a toilet, but walked down the corridor after Turnton. She passed one door that was open and she popped her head inside. It was a large room perhaps at the front of the house. The windows were blacked out, presumably with that film, she was thinking, as it was light inside. She could see everything that was there, in a dim light.

There were no pictures on the walls and no comfortable seating. There were deck chairs.

She found the Lord assembling items on a tray. It was then that Melia noticed there was nothing on the old dresser behind them, and on the table in front of them there were exactly three knives, forks and spoons, three plates -

And three mugs.

He was using two of them for coffee, made in the mug from a spoonful of 'Instant' from a jar. No cafetierre.

He opened a drawer in the table and took out a packet of biscuits. He counted two for each of them, and put them on one of the plates, then returned the nearly empty packet to the drawer.

"No cake. Sorry," he said with a smile, apologetically. "We will take it in the Library."

He picked up the tray and led her out of the kitchen and along the corridor, then turned right into the Library.

There were no books. In fact, there were no shelves, but there were a number of items covered in dust sheets that might have been furniture, or possibly boxes of books, not yet unloaded. After all, the Lord had only been in Salford a short time. Perhaps he simply hadn't had time to 'make himself at home'.

The chairs and table were the strangest that Melia had every seen. They were made from chicken wire, cut into cubes, with surfaces made from multicoloured, reprocessed plastic. The chairs weren't comfortable, even though they had arms and backs, and the table looked rather insecure, she was thinking, as the tray was put down on top of it.

Was this all he could afford, she wondered, or was he making a statement?

There was light in the room from the blackened windows. Melia went up close and looked through. They were at the back of the house, and she could see the lawn and a padlocked gate. Behind were trees and a path leading downhill.

"No sugar, I'm afraid," Lord Turnton said, to no one in particular.

"You'd better explain," Melia said, taking a seat and making the best of it. "Where have you come from?"

"Far up north. It all started with a visitor," he explained. "There was a knock on my door and there was a man in a suit and gumboots. He said he had a plan to blackmail Salford City Council. He advised me to resume my father's title and take up residence in the Manor House. He said he would make all the arrangements, and supply the furniture."

"It was him that took the boards off the windows and put up the black film?"

"Him and his gang."

Melia was baffled. "What did he look like? Where was he from? What else did he say?"

Turnton turned the questions over in his mind. "He was softly spoken, but he had a kind of Northern accent, like he might be from

Salford or Manchester. He didn't look like anybody much, very nondescript. He just laid out the plan."

"Which is? What do you have to do next?"

"I have to ask the Council for two million pounds," he said quietly. "I know. Ridiculous, right? Salford Council think they already own the place. Why would they want to buy it again? Anyway, it will cost them that much in renovation costs."

"You must be in touch with these people! Aren't you getting any further instructions?"

"They did say they'd be in touch, but so far, nothing."

He leaned out of his chair and took one of Melia's hands in his. He looked very young suddenly, very lost.

"Look, Melia," he said, "the fact is that I'd settle for ten per cent of that amount. I don't need much money, but I would like to buy a few more sheep. I could find them in Inverness at the market. It would make a big difference to my life."

"You can't go on like this!" Melia said, annoyed at his lack of forethought. He'd got money from this caller at his cottage door? Now it was all spent, and the flash car and shiny horse had gone.

It wasn't at all impressive for a dashing 'Prince'! What other revelations were there?

"Okay, I need help, I admit it," he told her. "You could do it. You're very strong-minded. Could we do a deal?"

She stared at him, horrified. No, she wouldn't jump on board a sinking ship, she decided.

Feeling the negativity in her stare, he jumped up. Melia saw that he was still wearing riding clothes.

"I need to get out of these jodhpurs," he announced. "Come with me. We can talk as we go. I'm sure you've got questions. Maybe there's things I haven't said, but I can explain. There's always an explanation for everything."

Melia was nervous about following the handsome man up to his bedroom, but she was just too curious. She wanted to see if the upstairs rooms were as empty as the downstairs. She didn't have to watch him dress, she was thinking - she could wait outside the door. Heavens, she was a grown woman. She was way past embarrassment!

They climbed the ornate staircase in the middle of the house and walked along an impressive balcony to a large room at the front of the house. Melia could see it was a bedroom, because there was a bed in it - of a sort. It was a black plastic blow-up double mattress, on the floor, with a few blankets and open sleeping bags on top.

Good Lord, she was thinking, it's like he's camping out!

Well, he certainly fooled me with his cut-glass manners and his upper-class accent. The little things!

The bedroom had more dust sheets covering items, big, like chests of drawers. Indeed they were. The Lord pulled back a sheet, opened a drawer and pulled out a pair of trousers.

No hangers? Melia was thinking. This really was slumming it, dear Lord! No wardrobes?

He sat down on the bed, struggled a little and looked perplexed. At last he spoke up.

"I'm going to need help getting these boots off," he said.

Melia was concerned too. Sure, she could help, but what if she hadn't been there? Who did he usually use?

She had to bend over, facing away from him and pull the boots away from her. Riding boots. Very heavy.

She ended up sprawling on the floor, in a very unladylike manner. Then do it all again with the left foot.

When she turned to face him, he was looking strangely thoughtful, as if something had just occurred to him.

He stood up gingerly on his stockinged feet, trying not to slip on the polished wood floor and went back to the chest of drawers. He pulled out another drawer and took out something small.

"Please sit, Melia," he asked politely and indicated the bed. Reluctantly she complied, not knowing what to expect.

He stood before her, then went down on one knee and brought his right fist out. It contained a ring.

"Marry me, Melia," he urged energetically.

There was a scuffle at the door.

Melia looked up to see two women standing there, obviously concerned by what was going on.

One was the cook/housekeeper Melia had met in the kitchen that last time she had gained entry to the Manor House. The other was a woman new to her, but other people would have been able to tell Melia that this person had been seen in the Conference Rooms the day the various property developers had been putting forward their proposals to the populace. The woman had introduced herself as the Lord's solicitor.

"What on Earth - " the 'solicitor' began, but Melia interrupted her, cutting her off in mid-flow.

"Who is this?" Melia demanded of the man. She was caught off guard for once in her life and it made her angry.

The Lord, trousers round his ankles, seemed embarrassed.

"This is my wife," Lord Turnton said sadly.

Chapter Twelve: Painting

"Who shot Al Gauze?" Caulfield said. "That is the question."

In order to try and answer that conundrum, the Deputy Director had worked with his colleagues in the Organised Crime Unit of Manchester City Police to invite all the gangs up to Buile Hill to do a spot of paint-balling.

It might have seemed unlikely it would happen - as the Police said at the time - but the gangs leapt at the chance of humiliating their rivals by splattering them in paint. Caulfield was quite clear in telling the gang leaders that this was instead of using real guns and bullets. They did seem disappointed, but were willing to call Truce for a day. Just one day only.

"We get them all in one place," Caulfield assured Chief Inspector Green, "and someone is bound to let information slip. We just have to keep our ears open."

"And our helmets on," the policeman said wryly.

Reluctantly, he had agreed that CID would provide a team for the tournament. It was like icing on the cake for the gangs. A chance to splat their rivals *and* the cops? Well, that was an opportunity you didn't get offered every day.

Caulfield checked the list on his clipboard.

The Hulme and Moss Side gangs, of course, and Al Gauze's 'A1 Team' were there. And locally? The Broughton Hillbillies; the XR Roosters; the Bury people, (who didn't seem to have a name); and the Monton Massive.

The only people who'd been invited but weren't showing up was the Village Gang. Someone said they hadn't been seen for months. Maybe they'd split up. the informant said. Well, we'll just have to manage, Caulfield concluded.

He was proud of how much he had achieved already.

The biggest hurdle had been trying to persuade Salford City Council to let them use the abandoned Depot in Buile Hill. It was perfect. The abandoned buildings, the derelict garage space and empty greenhouses. It was better than the forest, that was for sure. Some of the planners in the Council had suggested that paint-balling was usually held in wooded areas, but the Park Rangers were outraged at that. They'd spent years bringing the woods up to a good level. To have big, ugly criminals crashing through the undergrowth and splattering paint on their tree trunks? It was 'unthinkable', they said.

Caulfield had fully explored the Depot, (with the Council's permission).

He was pleased to see that when he opened up the old Office building, the water and power was still on. The place had toilets and a working kitchen, he told objectors. This is perfect. Besides, there were enough rooms upstairs that each gang could have its own changing area, to save their precious suits and leather jackets and put on the colourful armbands and tabards they would need to hunt each other down. Luckily, we've got enough different colours, he said, so each gang is different, easy to spot.

That was enough.

He was a little baffled that some of the buildings were 'off limits'. That was what he was told. But that was in terms of them not allowing him keys and being told to keep the marauding players on the outside. That was fine. It didn't occur to Caulfield that the injunction could be any kind of problem. The Depot was like a post-Apocalyptic urban landscape anyway. Really exciting. He was happy, standing by the gate, waiting for their arrival.

The Flower Fairy Parade was a surprise.

Nobody had told him that there might be a clash of users on the day. As far as he knew, the Paint-balling was the only thing booked and arranged to be going on. Wrong. There were dozens of young people and scores of parents.

Apparently, no one had told them they weren't supposed to be there, marching past the Caulfield in a line.

Amazingly, they were coming from the direction of the Manor House - but there was definitely nothing booked to be happening there! He had checked. However, from the look of things. this was all very well planned. Parents were lined up on the grass side of the access road, all the way up to the Main Gate. The parade of tots in fairy costumes emerged from the far side of the Manor House and moved slowly towards them, accompanied by a pipe band. There was cheering.

Caulfield crossed the road and asked one of the male adults for information.

"Sure, it's a new thing," he told Caulfield. "But it looks like Bonfire Night this year is being cancelled, and the Council's regular big firework display is off. What else we gonna do? This darn Covid crisis is ruining everything."

"There's still Trick and Treat," Caulfield said, hoping they might finish up the Parade early and leave him in peace.

"That's for the older kids," the man said, staring at him oddly. "This is for the preschoolers."

Looking along the line, Caulfield could that that was true. The average age was definitely Munchkin.

"Are the schools involved at all?" Caulfield asked, worried that 7 to 11's were missing out.

"Sure, they're following the band," his informant told him. "Look for the Headteacher at the front."

Caulfield did look for him, a familiar face, but didn't see him.

What he did see, at the front of the various bands of Flower Fairies - who were all dressed in wonderfully colourful costumes, with wings and halos - was a strange, tall man in a dark cloak and an unusually pointed hat.

At the back of the next age group, just behind the band, came a man on a brown horse. It was Lord Turnton.

He looked good. Caulfield wasn't surprised to see the alleged 'Lord of the Manor' would be taking a leading role, or, at least, a role in the lead. He didn't know that the Lord's identity was being questioned, or that he'd recently lost a horse and had been forced to replace it at short notice.

No, these facts were known only to Caulfield's colleague Melia, and the pair hadn't met up for weeks.

It was a bright and colourful display and, of course, the front runners didn't continue straight ahead when they were near the gate. They turned abruptly left, down the slope, parallel to the main road. They were turning back on themselves and heading back towards the Manor House. The proud parents ran across the lawns to 'head them off', so they could have a second look at their beloved offspring as they passed by for a second time.

That suited Caulfield. The kids were on the other track, heading away, by the time the gangs' many cars arrived at the main gate. The police greeted them, to make sure they didn't drive too fast, and ushered one way only - into the Depot and parking up in rows on the left hand side of the slope, on the hard-standing.

The bad guys clambered out of their limousines and assembled into their groups, staring out their rivals, and looking mean. They weren't given time to get into arguments, but were ushered into the old office building - through a hastily erected metal detector, which Border Force had lent to Manchester CID. It was necessary; many individuals were carrying guns, knives and knuckle dusters. Luckily, the Police weren't there to prosecute for that. They just made sure that fatal weapons were dropped into clear plastic bags, labelled with the name of the owner and put into a cupboard, The guys were told they could pick up their toys on the way out. This wasn't a problem, not today.

Then the gangs were ushered up the stairs to their assigned rooms, each with a clear notice on the door, listing their names.

Chief Inspector Green was smiling.

"All very smooth," he beamed at Caulfield. "A very well-run operation."

But then it was time for the game.

The gangs were released into the Depot, one colour at a time, with minutes between them. That did mean that the first out had the advantage of being able to find places to hide before the others erupted, but it was soon clear that none of the participants had anything like a plan. They fanned out, hid behind walls and around corners, but then simply waited. As soon as anyone from the opposition came along, the man with the paint ball gun would rush out and shoot, as hard and as fast as he could.

The Inspector commented: "I still would have preferred lasers."

It was true that lasers would have meant less mess, and a more accurate count of hits, but Caulfield was a bit old-fashioned about the contest. We will line them up, he assured the policeman, at the end of the time allowed, and it will be obvious who has been splatted least. It's only a game, Inspector, he said quietly.

The more important thing was the interactions along the way.

It was true. Bringing people into close contact like this - people who rarely saw each other close up, except when fighting - gave plenty of opportunities for ribald conversations, complaints and thrashing out of grievances. Even though the teams were partly hidden behind plastic masks, they still managed to identify those they liked and those they didn't. Caulfield was smiling at his cunning. There was a lot of business going on, he could see that, in between the goop.

The Rules stated that anyone could take a break in the office building whenever they wanted, where tea and biscuits, toilets and changes of guns and ammo, were available. That was genius. There was even more 'interaction' there.

However, the ages of the combatants ranged from teenager to retirees, and the older ones started to flag first.

The Captain of the yellow team, approached Caulfield at the door of the building, and announced that he'd had enough. He sat on a chair in the front room and allowed a policeman to serve him a mug of tea while he started peeling off his protective gear, layer by layer. His arms were covered in green slime. He took off a glove and started wiping it away.

The he fell off his chair.

"What's happening here?" the Chief Inspector demanded.

"Don't go near him!" Caulfield yelled, desperately reaching for his mobile phone.

He'd spotted, almost at once, that the man had developed red blotches all over his face.

Caulfield had seen something like that before, when he was working in Hong Kong.

He got Terry on the line. The kid was back in Regional Office, and was irritated at being disturbed, but when he heard the story and was allowed to see the victim, via the phone's camera, he was as sure as Caulfield.

"It's some kind of nerve agent!" Terry could be heard yelling. "Get everyone away from him! If it's the green gunk, then everyone with even a trace of it on them will need hosing down. Now! Don't let it take hold."

The Chief Inspector didn't need to be told twice. He ordered all his staff out of the room and told them to isolate anyone with green on their body, or on their protective armour, and corral them into groups.

"And don't touch it!" he shouted. "We need the HAZMAT team here now. Call Control!"

Still, there was one thing he was curious about, and he realised he didn't want to leave it, just in case.

He leaned over the man on the floor, the one with the yellow costume, and whispered something.

"Who did this to you?" he asked. "You must know something. Threats? Old scores to settle? Who?"

The man, the first of those affected, was in no doubt. Even though he was struggling to breathe, he pushed himself up on one elbow and stared at the uniformed policeman, happy to give him the facts, as far as he knew them.

"The Fairies did this to me," he said, through gritted teeth, then collapsed back onto the dirty floor.

Chapter Thirteen: Nothing

There is no Chapter Thirteen.

Chapter Fourteen: Folk Tale

Marilyn went to bed early so she wasn't asleep when there was hammering on the front door.

She staggered down the stairs in confusion, fearing the worst. Had the Manor House burned down? Was there a flood, a burglary, a car crash? It certainly sounded urgent. She was expecting to see a fire fighter, or a policeman.

She wasn't expecting a suave, darkly handsome man in a dinner jacket.

"Marilyn," he said, with a winning smile. "I've been told all about you. It's a pleasure to meet."

He had an American accent. Here? In Salford? It made no sense. He looked like - like -

"I'd be honoured," he said, as if he expected nothing more than acquiescence, "if you had dinner with me."

"It's late," she burbled, confused and flattered at the same time, almost lost for words.

"Actually, it's not," he told her, his voice quiet but firm.

"I'm not dressed," she said truthfully, thinking of the thin nightdress and silky dressing gown she was wearing.

"Where we're going," he told her, "I'd say you are ideally dressed."

"No, really - "

"Come as you are. Don't worry. Air conditioning and central heating every step of the way."

He took a step backwards and showed Marilyn a very large car, large, long and black, waiting by the kerb.

She said: "I'm only wearing slippers."

He said: "Then you are indeed a Fairy Princess."

The offer was tempting, and the only real problem for Marilyn was the thought that some of her nosey neighbours on the other side of the street might be looking out of their windows right now. They would disapprove, she knew.

Get a grip girl, she told herself. I don't know what the heck is going on, but this is an offer too good to miss.

Anyway, she was thinking, maybe I actually went to sleep just now, and this is all a dream, anyway.

"I don't even know your name," she said over her shoulder, as she swept down the steps and into the car.

"I'm Cyril Corsh," he told her. "You might not know me, but I'm sure you know my family, probably well."

He climbed in behind her and they nestled down in luxurious leather upholstery. He tapped on the window in front of him and the car pulled smoothly away. It was almost silent. An electric stretch limo? Was that even a thing now?

Corsh, she was thinking, mulling it over. Sure, she knew. The biggest property development company in the whole of the North West of England. The sort of firm she had often thought could sponsor her Manor House re-build.

Would that be possible - if she was particularly nice to this latest inheritor of the family business?

That's what he must be, she reasoned.

She didn't know him, never heard of him, but the Corsh Empire had a history of losing their figureheads and then having to bring in distant relations from far-off shores. The last one was Canadian, she was thinking. What happened to him?

"Where are we going?" she asked politely.

"Up to the top of Buile Hill," he told her.

That was a surprise. She had kind of assumed he was taking her to some fancy restaurant, not her daily stamping ground.

"You're American?" she asked brightly, hoping to at least get some background.

"Chicago," he told her. "I've developed my own business there. People call us The Chicago Mob, but I'm sure it's all in jest. I have interests in Denver also, but those connections are mainly handled by my Business Manager."

He waved a hand forward, pointing at someone sitting in front, next to the driver.

"Mr Smithers," Corsh said. "At least, that's what I call him. He is my Right Hand Man, after all."

"Will I meet him?" Marilyn asked, as if conducting a Due Diligence investigation.

"Dear Lady, you can meet whomsoever you desire. All will become clear. Just give me an hour of your precious time."

That hardly seemed long enough for dinner, Marilyn was thinking, suddenly realising she was loving this game.

They reached Eccles Old Road and swung in through the familiar entrance. The Manor House was on the left as the driver slowed along the access road. Mr Corsh was looking off to the right. Something on the lawn?

It was a helicopter.

The huge car came to a halt, and a man jumped out of the front and opened the back door for Marilyn.

He was wearing a sports coat and a flowery tie. His hair was cut short. He had glasses.

Mr Corsh had come round the other way and offered a hand to Marilyn, to help her out of the plush seat.

"Follow us in the car, Smithers," Corsh ordered, "in case I need your help later."

He gave Marilyn a dazzling smile, visible in the lights from the parked helicopter.

"Of course, I don't suppose I shall," he said gallantly, as Marilyn took his arm.

He can fly a helicopter, she was thinking. Of course he can! Why did I ever doubt he could?

The chauffeur got there first. He opened one side door for Marilyn, the honoured female guest, and showed her how the safety belts worked. He also picked up the headset, earphones and microphone, tapping them to test.

Corsh had gone round the other side of the aircraft and did his own strapping. He tapped his headphones and she heard his low tones in her ears. They wouldn't have to shout, she was thinking. This was perfect communication.

"Winter Hill Air Traffic Control, this is Corsh APD3, ready for take-off," he said, not to her.

It was all a blur for Marilyn. They seemed to leap into the air.

He must have filed a Flight Plan, she was thinking, as if her brain knew what was happening. In fact, it was all going so fast, she still couldn't be sure she was awake. This is like a dream, she thought, except it made perfect sense.

She was the Chair of The Friends of Buile Hill Manor House. He wants something from me, she was thinking.

"Where are we going?" she asked out loud, and the message was smoothly communicated.

"The Peak District," he told her. "I know a little restaurant - "

"Won't they be closing?"

"They'll stay open for me," he told her, and smiled at his own cleverness.

He was tapping dials, twisting little knobs and levers. Just as well, she was thinking. If he goes unconscious now, I won't have the slightest idea what to do. I am totally reliant on this man, his skills and his training.

There was a half moon visible, so some light shone down on the hills of Cheshire. They had left the city area so swiftly, she was lost when there was only the occasional small lights from farmhouses and cottages below.

She saw a twisting ribbon of silver below them, between an avenue of trees. It was the canal.

"You've done this run before?" she asked him.

He smiled at her, but wouldn't reply.

Please, please, she was thinking, tell me you know the way! Reassure me you've practised the route.

He seemed so supremely confident that she couldn't dent his good nature or his happy smile. She just had to hang on, and yes, they came swinging in, around a series of wind turbines, and settled into an isolated field.

Mr Corsh let the engine calm down and fade. He himself stopped. He seemed to be waiting for something.

When there was a tap on her door, Marilyn nearly jumped out of her skin. She wasn't expecting Ground Crew.

"For you," he said calmly, and indicated she should pull the exit lever.

The door swung open and she was faced with two burly men. They were carrying a plank between them.

"It's a muddy field," one said gruffly and told her to turn and lean back.

It's not dignified, Marilyn was thinking, slung between two peasants, but it saved her shoes and clothes and got her right up to the back door of the restaurant. Corsh followed. He had got some rubber boots from somewhere.

The place was deserted.

"No other customers?" she said, questioning.

"You can pick any table you like," he told her.

The tables at the front were up a couple of steps to a platform that gave a magnificent view down the valley, illuminated by moonlight and the occasional street lamp. There were hills on either side and behind them. It was a magical spot.

A waiter brought a menu, but that just confused her.

Mr Corsh said: "Tell the Chef we'll try everything."

Marilyn finally began to realise how much money this new Corsh in town was spending on her.

Was she worth it?

When the first bottle of wine arrived, she was happy to have a glass, mainly to hide her nervousness.

Then the food began to arrive. Small plates, small portions, but each tiny mouthful was exquisite and delightful. She couldn't deny the deliciousness. I could get used to this, she was thinking. But would she get the chance?

An hour flew by, and then she saw the big car come into the car park and swing around the side of the building.

"Mr Smithers will eat in the kitchen," Corsh assured her, as if it was some kind of running joke.

"Will you fly me back?" she asked him quietly, her voice husky from the wine.

"Your choice," he told her. "Air or road, whichever you prefer."

I prefer the High Life, she was thinking, if only I knew what I had to do to deserve it.

"The helicopter will suit me fine," she said, ready for the next course.

When the waiter came with the tray, Corsh told him: "Please inform Mr Smithers he needs to leave and meet us there."

The man nodded.

Two, Marilyn was thinking. There's two of them, or is it three? Plus the chef. Plus kitchen staff. Cleaners? Lots of them!

Her brain was becoming befuddled, but her host was quiet, attentive, charming. Mainly he talked about Britain. He wanted to know everything. What was it like to live here? How did people treat you? What should he expect?

Another hour passed and she was ready to go. Full, drowsy, she was glad to climb back into the helicopter, (with the help of the burly men) and close her eyes while Corsh fired up the engine and took them smoothly into the air.

"I'm glad we took this choice," he told her. "I'll be able to show you the building site."

That rang alarm bells for Marilyn, but he wasn't talking about the top of Buile Hill, he was talking about the bottom, the maze of small streets off Liverpool Road. He lowered the helicopter delicately down into the middle of an empty plot that was surrounded by roadside boards.

"In two weeks, this whole area will be crawling with builders, machinery and scaffolding," he told her.

A Corsh project? Building here? She hadn't even noticed a Planning Application.

"Will you support it?" he asked.

She had no reason to disapprove. It didn't intrude in any way into her plans for the Manor House.

He seemed pleased.

"Then I have a Job Offer for you," he told her. "You finish the Manor House here, and then I'll pay you to work on another place for me. It's called Dirtdale Clough and it's in Tameside. I'll give you a hundred thousand per year."

Marilyn might have gasped or protested, but she was feeling too sleepy to respond adequately.

"I don't expect an answer," he said. "Not now. Let me know your thoughts, in your own good time. No rush."

There was the soft beep of a car horn from outside. It was Corsh's large limousine.

"I only live two hundred yards from here," she protested.

"And I couldn't possibly allow you to walk," he told her, still bright, still smiling. "Smithers will see you safely home."

As she started to clamber out, a stray thought came to Marilyn. Yes, she should put it out there.

"Have you got any plans for Buile Hill?" she asked, a little tentatively.

"We can discuss that later," he said smoothly.

Chapter Fifteen: Relations

"Hello, Auntie Mel," the girl said when Melia opened the door to her flat.

Melia froze in horror.

"Em?" she said quietly. Her sister's kid?

"I've run away from home," the youngster informed her Aunt. "I need somewhere to stay."

The girl had nothing but the clothes she stood up in and a small rucksack. It was getting dark. It was winter. Of course Melia let her in, no matter how shocking this surprise visit was. Emma was family. Melia needed to respond.

Even if she hadn't seen the girl's mother in twenty years. There was no communications between them.

Melia said: "Clear the couch and sit down. I'll put the percolator on and we'll have coffee."

"You know I don't drink tea?"

I haven't been stalking you, or anything, Melia was thinking awkwardly, but I have seen you on Social Media.

I'm your Godmother, Em. I do have certain responsibilities.

Melia came back into the Lounge with a tray and put it on the low table. She waited for the coffee to brew.

"I couldn't move this bag," Her niece told her, indicating the heavy sports bag at the end of the settee.

"What's in it?" she asked her Aunt.

"One hundred thousand pounds," Melia said quietly, hoisted the bag and slung it into the corner.

Should she bother to explain? Her boss, Richard Caulfield, had asked her to get the cash for an operation he was involved with. When Melia asked him what it was for, he said, mysteriously: "I need to buy some drugs."

Melia was hoping he didn't mean that literally, and it was just some kind of undercover 'sting'.

You never knew with Caulfield.

Melia poured hot coffee into mugs and let her niece add cream and sugar. She watched the girl relax.

Then she got tough.

"I've a bedroom to spare, Em," Melia told her with a smile. "You can stay as long as you like. Short-term, until this latest spat works out. Or long-term. I'll help you find a place in Manchester if you want one, but there's one condition."

Her niece wouldn't meet her eyes, as if she knew Melia would come up with a rule or two.

Melia said: "Pull out your phone, now, and text your Mother to tell her you are warm and safe. You can tell her you're 'staying with friends', or any lie you like. Just reassure her - Oh, and don't mention me."

Emma gave her a look. Melia could guess what that meant. 'You're worried about the woman you haven't spoken to since before I was born? What kind of sister are you?'

Her niece started at her, but Melia was better at not blinking, and she won the contest.

Emma pulled out her phone and tapped out a message. It bleeped almost immediately in reply.

"I'm not getting into a dialogue," the girl said, flinging the phone onto the coffee table.

Melia sipped her coffee. "You wanna talk?" she asked, concerned but not demanding.

"Not right now," the girl said, in a good act of not being bothered.

"When you're ready," Melia agreed.

Melia wasn't going to force her niece to do anything. She could only imagine the kind of hell that Em was escaping. If anything, the biggest surprise was that the visitor hadn't arrived years before, seeking sanctuary.

I'll do whatever I can, she thought silently. I owe you something, Em. Maybe I ruined your life

"I'd be more happy to talk about one hundred thousand pounds," Emma said quietly. "You lead such an exciting life, Auntie Mel. You know that's why Mum hates you, don't you? Are you going to spend the money tonight?"

Melia shook her head. She was waiting for Caulfield to call, but that might be days away.

Right then, there was a knock on the door.

Emma looked fearful.

Perhaps she thought her family had found her. Perhaps she thought they'd called in the Police.

Melia went over and opened her apartment door. There weren't many people who could get up the stairs without having to ring the outside bell. Just a few friends and relatives.

"Relax," Melia told her niece when she saw who it was. "He's just a policeman."

Melia went to fetch another mug for Don, and he sat on the other easy chair. interested but relaxed.

When Melia came back from the kitchen she noticed that Emma was sat on the edge of the sofa, like a scared rabbit, fixed in the headlights and ready to run. Everyone needed to calm down, she was thinking.

She sat in her previous position and said: "Don, this is my niece, Emma from Bristol. She's here on a visit."

He nodded, gave her a polite smile. Sure, they needed to be introduced.

"Em, this is Don Fellowes. He's engaged to your Auntie Liv, my cousin who lives in Salford. They've got a flat together on the University Campus now, I think. Anyway, he's a Detective Sergeant in Manchester CID."

"Auntie Liv?" Emma said, in wonder. She hadn't heard that name in a long time.

Melia smiled. "If we ever get organised and have a Family get-together, I'm betting that Don will be the Black Sheep of the family. Am I right? It's Liv that's done the best for herself, isn't it? She's almost respectable."

"What are you doing now, Auntie Mel?" Emma asked innocently. Her mother told her nothing.

"Oh, you know, the usual. I'm just a middle manager in Information Admin," she lied.

"I need your help, Melia," Don said urgently.

Melia flashed him a glance. There was plenty she wasn't telling her niece, she wanted to say.

He thought a bit about what he would say, how it might fit Melia's recently concocted cover story.

He said: "Maybe you can confirm the rumours, Melia. Have you spotted any internet chatter about Buile Hill recently? Our informants are telling us there's drugs coming from direction. It makes no sense! The Manor House is waiting for renovation, and the Depot has been empty for years. Could it be the Conference Rooms, do you think?"

Melia took a few breaths. "If people were talking on the web, our team would spot it," she said, as if agreeing she had access to Intel. "Don't worry, Don, I'm happy to help. I'll go in tomorrow morning and put the flags up. Maybe we've missed something. If there's anything there, you'll be the first to know."

Emma was impressed by this grown-up interchange and kept quiet while they did their business. She didn't want to spoil the flow by asking silly questions. She would get the whole story soon, she figured, after Don left.

She was wrong.

Detective Don stay for nearly an hour, but the only thing he talked about was his planned wedding to Auntie Liv. Now that he had found out little Emma existed and was a bona-fide member of the family, he was happy to invite her.

"I'll make sure you get a proper invitation," he enthused, happy to include her.

"Give it to me," Melia told him, "and I'll pass it on."

"And your sister?"

Melia looked pained and didn't answer at first, so Emma jumped in.

"Oh, Mum finds it difficult to travel," she said lightly. "I'm sure she'd be thrilled to be invited but she probably won't be able to come. It's nice of you to ask me. I've never met Auntie Liv in the flesh, but she's sent me Birthday Cards."

Don had no comment, as if he wasn't surprised by Melia's complicated family. He was marrying Liv, not the rest.

After he'd gone, Emma jumped right in, as if eager to clear things up.

"You told him nothing!" she said quietly, putting Melia on the spot.

Melia paused. So much like her mother, she was thinking. Always calling me to account.

She said: "Em, I'll provide the bed and facilities, but if you want explanations, you'll have to wait."

Emma was stopped in her tracks. Auntie Melia was pleasant enough, she thought, but she has a heart of steel.

She wasn't going to argue.

There wasn't much room for small talk. Melia was unwilling to discuss the past, and so Emma did her best to update her Aunt, on school, college. Her hobbies. But when she mentioned music, the two women soon found they had absolutely no interests in common. They were a completely different generation.

Emma said: "I want to come to Manchester for a University. The night life is amazing, I'm told. So many bands, such good vibes. What do you think, Auntie Melia? Do you think I'd fit in?"

Melia smiled. If Emma came to the University, then they would supply the bedroom, she was thinking.

That's the way she would prefer it. Polite, but slightly distant.

"I need my sleep," she told the young girl.

Emma said she wanted to watch television, but there was a set in the spare bedroom. She also had her own bathroom. Em smiled, thanked her Aunt and said she would see her in the morning. She went in and shut the door.

Melia moved the mugs and plates away, took one last look around and went to bed.

It was gone midnight when she heard the front door quietly open and close.

Melia jumped out of bed, worried, but she didn't need to. The door to the guest room was empty and it was slightly ajar. There was a side light on and nobody in the bed. Melia thought she might have run away, then noticed the rucksack in the corner. No, Emma hadn't moved on, just taken some time out.

Also, taken Melia's door keys from the hook in the kitchen. And some money, from the Sports Bag.

It was past 3am when the door opened again and Emma walked in, a little flustered and rather sweaty.

"You didn't have to worry about me," she told her Aunt. "I was able to find my way around."

Melia reassured her she wasn't worried, and let her go off to bed without a cross word of recrimination.

"You're really cool, Auntie," Emma told her, then pulled a wrapped bundle of bank notes from the inside pocket of her smart leather jacket. "I only spent less than a hundred," she reported, and tossed the remainder back in the bag.

"Good Night," she said, suppressing a yawn.

"Good Night, Emma, sleep well," Melia said, and meant it. She wished her every happiness.

Melia wasn't annoyed.

She looked at the sports bag with its zip pulled back and the wads of notes showing. I've got some cash, Melia was thinking. I'll make the amount up, she thought to herself, and no one will notice the difference.

It's not a problem, Em, she was thinking.

I owe you that much, at least.

Chapter Sixteen: Folk Tale

Caulfield was in the hospital, waiting for the sleeping man to wake up.

The Deputy Director had been pacing the room, bored out of his mind. For hours, he only had himself for company and it was driving him mad. When he agreed the request from Mr Gibson to monitor this refugee from Melia's coffin delivery, Caulfield had a vision of a bustling hospital ward, medical personnel running to and fro, fighting emergencies.

He had no idea the man had been shoved into a side ward, on his own, and there was no bustling. Nothing.

When he arrived, a Consultant had said to Caulfield: "There's a red button there. If the situation changes in any way, give it a push and we'll be alerted." Caulfield nodded. He was capable of that, at least. He'd cope, he thought.

"Won't you be monitoring him?" he asked the medic, suddenly realising he might have no company.

"The nurses will checks his vitals at change of shift. Meanwhile the machines monitor everything else."

I should have brought a book, Caulfield was thinking now.

He had his phone with him, but when he pulled it out, the Doctor gave him a very disapproving look.

"It might interfere with the machinery, Old Pal," he said, patronisingly. "We wish you wouldn't."

Was that an order? Caulfield now, three hours later, was willing to break a few rules, just for some interaction.

There was a TV, but the plug had been taken out. Were they worried the burble of television would alarm the man in the coma? Maybe it was something about his dreams, they didn't want to provoke anything. He needed to rest, maybe.

Like that man in the Fairy Story, Caulfield was thinking. The one who slept for a hundred years.

Yes, when this guy wakes up, he won't know what day it is. He might not even remember what happened to him. Apparently. That was the best the doctors could come up with. The patient had been frozen in the belly of the aircraft. He had an oxygen tank with him, they knew that, but he could have been deprived of air. His brain might be damaged.

Caulfield, still mulling, did the only other thing he could think of - he went out to talk to the policeman.

There was one outside the door.

That would have been fine, if they'd been allowed to co-operate. But Caulfield was from TEEF, the anti-terrorism unit, and the copper was just a humble constable from Manchester Police Division. They had separate bosses.

"How about a coffee?" Caulfield suggested, poking his head out of the door.

"Sure," the younger man said, "but are you allowed to leave the suspect? What are your orders?"

You want me to fetch the coffee? Caulfield was thinking, shocked. Surely I'm the superior officer!

"Can't you leave your post?" Caulfield asked. "I can watch the patient."

"That's your job," the copper agreed, "but my job is to stand out here and make sure no bad guys come along and try and do him some damage. If you think you could do my job - Have you got a gun?"

Caulfield was shocked again. No, he wasn't carrying a firearm. He really hadn't thought he would need it!

I'm floundering, he realised.

I should have listened closer to the Briefing. Not just Gibson, but Terry the technician got involved in setting the scene.

It seems that the techs had managed to get fingerprints off the guy and run them through a number of databases. He popped up on Interpol. He wasn't a 'bad guy', he was a journalist, but he had been arrested multiple times, in countries as far apart as Israel, the Congo, and now Afghanistan. Nobody was saying he was a threat and needed to be contained - as far as British Intelligence knew - but he had sure upset a few regimes in his time.

That's why the policeman was there - to keep him alive long enough for him to answer some searching questions. If he had logical answers, he probably wouldn't be charged with anything. Entering the country in a coffin wasn't really a crime - just yet - but only because he was a British National. Any other passport holder might have been ejected.

Caulfield had to admit that he wasn't that keen to drink coffee - especially the sludge on offer in this wing of the hospital - but he still needed some activity to keep him sane. He tried to think it through.

"Listen," he said, trying to sound authoritative, "you fetch the coffees and I'll take your place. That's the important job, right? Keeping the assassins at bay? I'm sure the man in the bed isn't going to wake up on my watch."

The young man didn't seem convinced. Certainly, Caulfield seemed the more experienced man - he had spent years in the Hong Kong police, but hadn't mentioned it yet, in conversation - but there was an air of cutting corners about the man, riding close to the boundaries. He seemed as though he liked to have his own way.

Taking a deep breath, not wanting to argue, the policeman said: "I'm going to have a muffin with it."

"Sounds great," Caulfield told him. "Make mine the same. Oh, and put it on expenses."

He pulled a twenty pound note from his pocket and pressed it into the surprised young man's hand.

"I'll - uh - I'll get a receipt," the cop assured him.

The youngster walked off up the corridor, and Caulfield was as good as his word, and took his place. This was better, he was thinking. Much more life here, more lively. He could see people passing by. He felt a link to the world.

There was a buzzing noise.

Caulfield was enjoying himself too much to pay it much attention, at first, but it occurred to him that the sound wasn't coming from his phone. He looked up. There was a red light over the door and it was flashing.

Slowly, as if waking up and being dragged from his bed, Caulfield realised what might be causing the alarm. He rushed back into the room. Sure enough, the patient in the bed had his eyes open and was trying to raise himself on his elbow.

"Where am I?" he croaked, his voice thick with disuse.

"Salford," Caulfield assured him. "North West England."

"I made it," the man said, and seemed overcome with relief. "I made it, I made it. What about the others?"

Caulfield was stunned.

He'd assumed that the story would be that the man had been put in a coffin to allow him to escape the chaos of the country, and had been smuggled in a batch of coffins with genuine corpses.

Why would anyone else not be dead?

The journalist saw Caulfield's confusion. He didn't know who this man in a suit was, but he was guessing he was plain clothes Police, or maybe British Security. Didn't they know the plan? Hadn't Kabul communicated with Salford?

He said: "Twenty coffins. Four people alive, sixteen dead."

Caulfield shook his head.

No, that didn't seem right. There were a lot more than twenty total, according to Melia, and -

"Everyone else was dead," he blurted out. "Sorry. I mean, I don't know who you were expecting - "

"Colleagues," the man said vaguely. "We all had Intel. We were valuable. The Russians said they would take care of us."

Why on Earth would they do that, Caulfield was thinking? His stupid expression betrayed him.

"We had been investigating the Americans," the man said. "Corruption, and all that. It's explosive data."

"You don't need to go into that now," Caulfield said, unthinking. "Now they've pulled out."

The man seemed more and more alarmed. He tried harder to raise himself up, though it was only making him weak.

"So who's supporting the government now?"

"The Afghan government? It's all Taliban. You don't know that? Anything? Anything about that?"

The man collapsed back onto his pillow, as though all the life had been sucked out of him. He was breathing heavily.

"It's all happened in the last few months," Caulfield said, trying to be gentle. "You weren't aware what happened?"

"I was four months in House Arrest," the journalist said, "then two months in hiding, with no TV, no internet. They smuggled me to the airport in the dead of night. No, I know nothing about recent developments."

Caulfield, looking for a place to put his foot in it, said: "I suppose your important Intel might be a little out of date."

Date? The young man wanted to know what date it was, and when Caulfield told him, he sighed again.

"In a coma for weeks?" he said, disbelievingly. "I thought I had enough oxygen - "

"Maybe they were trying to kill you," Caulfield said helpfully.

"How long has this light been on?" a medical man demanded, rushing into the room.

"Oh, he's woken up," Caulfield assured the man in the white coat. "He seems very alert."

The Doctor began checking readings and tapping the patient for reactions.

He told the victim: "You were in an aircraft hold for nearly twenty four hours, as far as we can estimate. We've been warming you up slowly. Too fast and we would have shocked your brain into shut-down. It seems to have worked."

"Thanks, Doc," the man in the bed said. "You know, Salford was our first choice. It's a direct flight, and they say that the medical care is second to none. Sorry to give you so much trouble. I thought I would have woken up long ago."

The Doctor seemed flattered, but appeared to have no idea who the man was, so Caulfield told him.

"He's a journalist," he said, forgetting there might be such a thing as 'secrets'. "He was investigating people."

"It's all about drugs, in Afghanistan," the patient said, trying to shut Caulfield up. "The Drug Lords hate me. Me and a few friends. We found out way too much about their connections, here and in the Middle East."

The Doctor perked up at that.

"What happened to your friends?" he asked, knowing that this man was his only patient.

"Oh, we don't know too much about that," Caulfield said, saying too much again. "I'll ask my colleagues."

The patient said: "I was promised oxygen. We all were. Looks like we got double-crossed. Again."

"Not just that," the Doctor said. "If they didn't have the layers of survival bags you had, they wouldn't have survived. Sorry, but what you did - or they did - was incredibly risky. Lots of thing could have gone wrong."

The victim seemed to grit his teeth. "I got this far," he said. "Maybe now I can tell my story - "

The door banged open.

Caulfield turned and saw a posse of men in suits. Behind them, the lone policeman looked worried but ineffective. He was carrying cups of coffee in both hands - not an ideal position to think about drawing your gun.

"We take over from here!" the front man said. "Stand down, Mr Caulfield. You've done enough."

Caulfield was too pompous and self-important to be swept away so easily.

"Show me credentials," he demanded. "Where are you from? Who do you represent?"

"Would you believe CIA?" the one on the right asked, smiling aggressively.

"Not with that accent!" Caulfield retorted. The man sounded Russian.

The first man said: "We have territorial rights granted by your British government. You may leave."

"I'll leave when I'm ordered to," Caulfield said petulantly. "Stay there while I call Head Office."

He pulled out his phone, and the Doctor gave him a frown, again. Rules were Rules.

"Not in here," he snapped. "Take your mobile phone outside the doors please."

Caulfield started to move, reluctantly.

"I'll go outside," he said to the Doctor, "but please do not allow these men to take the patient away."

The medic seemed outraged.

"He's my patient," he declared forcefully, "and he's going nowhere until I decide he's fit enough to move."

"That needs to be soon," the first man in the suit said, sarcastically.

The Doctor fixed Caulfield with a steely gaze.

"You'd better hurry," he advised the Deputy Director.

Chapter Seventeen: Trapped

"I want to come too!" Emma said to Melia.

Melia stared at her niece with concern. Lord, she was only a teenager! What did she know about spying, working undercover, facing down the bad guys? She was raw. Full of energy, but unskilled.

She didn't want to be taking risks.

"All right, Em," she said. "This is a piece of surveillance. I'm not expecting to meet anyone, and neither should you. If we bump into somebody, take my lead. If you're asked a question, say nothing, Got it?"

Emma nodded, pleased to be included. She was smiling happily, eager to be part of the team.

She had pulled her hair back and tucked it under a woollen hat. Melia nodded. It might be cold where they were going.

They were going back to the cellar of the Manor House.

Melia was annoyed that no one at Regional Office seemed to be interested in the missing coffins. She had tried to talk to Terry about it, but he gave the impression of being busied on all sorts of technical issues, which meant he couldn't give it another thought. That annoyed Melia. It was like having a mystery - unsolved. The job wasn't finished.

Then she had an idea.

Nobody in the Unit felt it was necessary to send in the Forensics team, so she would do her own. She would take pictures of the empty cellar and, who knows, they might find footprints in the dust. They could scour the rooms and look for any little items the intruders might have dropped, like keys or a credit card. That would do it! Identity established.

Actually, Melia had never had such luck in any former investigation. It was ridiculous.

Maybe she could find fingerprints. She had an ultraviolet flash-light -

Melia stopped worrying. She wanted to get out of the flat, and this was the first idea she could come up with. Also, she wanted Emma to get some exercise and see around Salford and Manchester. Accordingly, they went down to the basement of the apartment building and Melia fired up her little car. They drove out, around the City Centre, on to the A6 and The Crescent. Emma seemed impressed by Salford University. Maybe she would go there, Melia mused.

They turned off on to Eccles New Road and took the top entrance into Buile Hill park. Melia drove up the access road and parked in front of the Conference Rooms. There was nothing happening there, she could see.

They climbed out of the car and Melia scanned the grassy areas. Dog walkers, nothing more. Still, she waited for everyone to disappear from view before leading Emma to the side door of the Manor House.

"You've got a key?" the young girl said in wonder.

Melia tried to explain about Terry's little trick, but by that time she had the door open and they ducked inside.

Dark. Cold. Mysterious.

Full of coffins.

Melia swiftly closed the door behind them and snapped on her regular flash-light, indicating Emma should do the same.

"I thought you said it would be empty?" Emma whispered, too intimidated to raise her voice.

Melia was nodding, thinking hard. How could this happen?

The cellars were full. The cellars were empty. Now they were full again. How could that be?

"Okay, look," she hissed back. "I have no idea why this is. It's a surprise to me."

"You told me about the coffins," Emma complained. "You said they'd been moved out!"

"Right. This shouldn't be happening."

Melia had only one thought - she needed advice.

She looked at her niece beside her, and saw how confused the poor kid was - and scared. This was like one of those vampire films that the girl had told her she loved so much, but without the romance. This was just plain frightening.

Melia said: "Look, I need to phone Regional Office. I can't get get a signal in here. I'll have to go outside."

Emma nodded. "I'll be fine."

"You want to stay here?"

"Don't worry about me."

Melia was impressed by her fortitude. It was true that even if the boxes were full of bodies and drugs, they couldn't hurt her. But still - the teenager was putting on a good front and being brave. Melia liked it. She was a good kid.

Melia let herself out, carefully. If she had bumped into someone - even if it was only a person walking their dog - she'd have felt worried. She didn't want to be observed while she was working undercover. She wanted to be invisible.

She walked up to the trees, stood under one and made a phone call. She wanted information.

Terry didn't have any.

When she told him where she was and what she had just seen, he simply seemed baffled.

"I put trackers on those coffins," he said, "and I know where they went. Port Salford. They haven't gone back, I'm pretty sure of that. So there's only one explanation - a new delivery. I don't know when they arrived - "

"I thought we had Intel on the delivery!" Melia protested. "We knew when they arrived, where from - "

"Nothing about a second run," Terry insisted. "I mean, look, it's unlikely. The airport at Kabul was surrounded. The first consignment came out on one of the last planes allowed to fly. So who could put together a second collection, and get permission? As far as I can tell, there's no certification going on right now. The new government - "

"Maybe 'unlikely', but I know what I'm seeing," Melia said, a little too forcefully than she intended.

"Are the coffins full?"

Melia stopped. Oh, how stupid could she be? She hadn't checked! Coffins would be filled with bodies, right? But if this was a second time around, then all bets were off. Bodies? Maybe. Drugs? Maybe. Both? She didn't know.

"I'll phone you back," she said and snapped the phone off. She hurried back down the slight slope.

I'm going to have to open a few boxes, she was thinking. I hope it doesn't freak poor Emma out.

She needn't have worried.

Emma wasn't there.

Melia freaked. She looked under the stacks, along each wall. She called her name, gently. She went up to the door that led upstairs, but the bolts were firmly pulled shut. No one had gone through there, not with the bolts in place.

This couldn't be! Melia thought furiously, staggering out into the sunshine. Where on Earth had she gone?

Melia came back up the hill, looking around and around. She would have to ask someone, she thought reluctantly.

Such as the elves.

Coming around the corner of the Conference Suite, she saw a dozen children lined up in green uniforms. There were no adults around. They seemed to be waiting for something, but not in a distressed way. They were smiling.

"Who are you?" Melia asked. She couldn't help herself. It was all too absurd!

"We live here," the middle kid said helpfully, in slightly accented English. "We are Asylum Seekers, living in the attic. No one knows we are there. The Magician told us the bedrooms were created the last time the Suite was re-furbished."

"This place is for Conferences and weddings," Melia said, confused. "Dozens of people come and go. You mean no one has noticed you, ever? With all those comings and goings?"

Another child came forward. Melia didn't know it, but this was one of the Woodcutter's children.

"We serve at banquets," she said. "We are 'The Staff'. No one questions that."

"You're under-age workers!" Melia observed.

"We are slaves," the youngster agreed happily.

This was too much! But Melia had no time to stop and investigate. She had cellars to explain, and her ward missing.

"I'm looking for a young girl," she said. "Not as tall as me. Brown hair tuckled under a woollen hat."

"Oh, she escaped down the tunnel," the kid said, matter-of-factly. "She saw the Fair people coming and didn't want to be seen. We showed her a way out. You go down there and come out in the circular pond, at the bottom of the hill."

Melia looked up and, for the first time, noticed that there were caravans and lorries at the back of the grassy space, over towards the main road. Ah, a Funfair, she realised. The Council invited these people in to the park, maybe twice a year, usually on some celebration date. Like Halloween, for example.

"I need to find my niece," Melia said simply, looking for help.

The kids were happy to take Melia around the back of the building. There was a lawn there, in front of French windows. This was where people mingled at a Wedding Reception or Birthday party. It was all a bit cold for that today.

One of them showed her the metal cover in the corner, by the hedge. Some sort of manhole cover?

It took two of the youngsters to pull the cover back. Looking in, there was a metal ladder.

"This is the way we get to church," one of the kids said, in a foreign accent. "This way, we don't be seen."

Melia stared. Emma went down there? It didn't seem likely. She was nervous in cellars!

One of the elves said: "The girl, she was in panic. She seemed really scared about the Fair. We don't know why."

Melia hesitated, but not for long. She had to find Emma, so this was it: she would follow her track.

"Have you got a torch?" the tiny tots asked her.

Luckily, Melia was able to say that Yes, that was the one thing she did have.

She clambered down the ladder and saw a brick-lined tunnel in front of her, leading down. She was about to shout a 'Thank You' but the metal cover was clanged shut above her and there was now no light, apart from her torch.

It was cold, slippery, but surprisingly roomy. Melia didn't have to bend. If she stretched out her arms, her fingertips would find the walls on either side. The only question was why such an Escape Tunnel would exist here at all?

Perhaps it had something to do with the Second World War, Melia was thinking. At that time there were anti-aircraft guns installed on top of old Buile Hill, and searchlights and Barrage Balloons, to protect the Docks at the bottom of the hill, on the river. Strange things happened then, in the 1940s. Maybe this was a way to escape the bombs.

She carried on down for what seemed like a hundred yards and then the floor got dark. Melia looked closer.

It was water.

She was expecting a door, opening into the sump. That's what she had been told.

Melia's thoughts were racing. She couldn't believe that Emma would have tried to go through the water! Maybe it wasn't there, before. Maybe Emma walked through the tunnel and out the door, then left it open and water in the pond backed up. Something like that. Whatever happened, Melia was now faced by a pool of water, lapping at her feet.

She would have to swim out.

There was no going back. Whatever, Melia was thinking, Em was ahead of her. She needed to go on.

Taking off her shoes and tying them to her belt, taking off her jacket and tying it around her waist, she was as ready as she would ever be. She waded forward, into the water, then lowered herself gradually until she was under the freezing surface. One large gulp of air - would it be enough?

She didn't have to go far.

The water was over her head, but it was surprisingly clear. Rainwater then, it must be. Luckily, her flash-light was waterproof and shone steadily at what was ahead. A door. A metal door. There were two large cleats on the right hand side. The bolts were pulled across. The implications were hammering at her brain, but she had no time to debate it. She hauled the bolts open and threw her full weight against the door. It opened outwards, all in a rush, the water behind pushed Melia forward - forward into the pond. She ended sitting, looking up at the brick walls all around her.

Emma didn't come this way! she realised. She couldn't have opened the door then locked it from the inside.

I've been betrayed, she was thinking. They tried to kill me. Those little green people. Innocent looking? But deadly.

"Hello, again," a cheery voice said. "I thought I heard splashing but I didn't think it would be you, going for a swim."

It was a long story, Melia was thinking, not sure where to start and not really wanting to share.

It was the Housekeeper, the cookery lady from the Manor House. She held up a bag.

"I've been shopping for lunch," she said. "Come and join us. I might be able to find you some dry clothes."

Melia hauled herself up one of the brick walls and out of the sump. She was sopping wet.

But lucky to be alive.

Fortunately, the older woman wasn't interested in explanations. She walked up the hill with Melia, the back way, and happily chatted as they went along - describing the weather, her shopping expedition. The Lord? He was out, but coming back later to eat. She had to provide, and tidy the place up, she said.

"The Lady is about your size," she said. "I'm sure she'll have some jeans and sweaters around. I'm too small for you."

"The solicitor? His wife?" Melia asked, squelching along.

"Oh, sure. She does the legal stuff. I prefer playing house. It suits me. Short and dumpy, doing all the cooking."

"I need a warm shower," Melia said, shivering. "Any dry clothes would be welcome."

"Well, take your pick," the older woman said. "Oh, and your slipper is in the house. You might want that back."

Melia suddenly recalled where she had lost it. The Ball. Also, what the Lord said, next time she met him.

"He asked me to marry him," she blurted. What had come of that? She'd heard nothing from him.

"It might work," the woman said, not fazed. "But you'd be the third. What role would you prefer, in the house?"

"Now?" Melia asked, confused. "You're both married to him now? Or are you one after another?"

"Now," she confirmed. "Currently."

They walked along in silence for a while, until the cook suddenly turned to Melia.

"Just one thing," she said to Melia. "Don't get trapped, like us."

Chapter Eighteen: Folk Tale

"They call me Midas," Cyril Corsh said to Dirk Forrest, "because everything I touch turns to gold."

"I don't much care for money," Dirk said, honestly.

They were sitting outside the Pavilion in the lower part of Buile Hill park, the Seedley south side.

Dirk wasn't sure whether he'd actually invited Cyril, but the rich businessman may have invited himself, then. Either way, he came breezing into Dirk's area and insisting on buying the green-fingered community worker a cup of tea. Dirk tried to explain that the tea counter had a 'Pay as much as you want' policy, but that seemed to go right over Cyril's head.

Mr Corsh told his trusty aide, Mr Smithers, to sort out the details, then sat down under a tree, at one of the metal tables that had been put out for casual passers-by, as well as all the people who had allotment plots there and needed a break.

He sat opposite Dirk and demanded to know what the horticulturist had planned.

Dirk shuffled in his metal chair. Why the Inquisition? There were signs everywhere, information boards and photos of past events. Everybody who came into the gated area had the chance to read full details of what his project was all about.

"This is the Reception area," he explained. "Everyone is welcome. Users of the park, dog walkers, cyclists, they want a cup of something or the chance to use the toilet? That's what the Pavilion supplies. It's run by volunteers from The Friends of Buile Hill Park, and they are open when we are open, four days a week. That lawn behind us used to be the Bowling Club, but they collapsed years ago. It's used by the Croquet Club now, two afternoons a week. They are mostly the older generation, but they're anxious to get new members, especially younger people, and you are welcome to join the Club, or just have a game, and give it a try. They play Golf Croquet, which is a variation on the older game. They're very competitive."

"So am I," Cyril Corsh whispered, as if in full approval.

Smithers arrived with a tray. There were cups of hot water, teabags, milk cartons and sugar packets.

Dirk said: "Sorry, you have to mix your own tea. I suppose you could get this man to do it for you."

He was trying to be humorous. Neither of his guests saw a joke around. Mr Corsh waved his assistant away.

He said: "You haven't told me about your section, Dirk."

Dirk Forrest, impressed that 'Mr Midas' opposite him, was capable of putting his own teabag into water, said: "The area on your right, down that slope, is where the second Bowling Green used to be. About ten years ago I was employed by a mental health charity called 'Going Places' to organise a group of people into being gardeners. We erected a series of raised beds and planted flowers and vegetables. We put fruit trees round the edges and bramble fruits on the railings. One of the group was an excellent woodworker, and he built a large pergola in the middle of the plot."

Dirk paused to sip his tea.

He looked at his interlocutor. Mr Corsh was rolling his eyes. The message was clear. 'I could really have made this place pay,' he was thinking. He was building a picture of Dirk Forrest as being a very inefficient businessman.

"Then what happened?" he said slyly, as if he already knew the answer.

Dirk said: "The charity ran out of grant money and made all the staff redundant. We kept it going for a few months, but people drifted away. After that, the gates were locked and it was deserted for a few years."

"Then you came back?"

Dirk considered. Yes, he came back. He had been working at another project, in South Central Manchester, but that fell through too. He was at a loose end. He came back to visit Buile Hill park, got to know some of 'The Friends' and talked to the Croquet Club. Nobody minded if he made another attempt to get people planting and growing.

Mr Corsh smiled. "Why did it work this time? You had no money! No grants, no cash."

"I think the pandemic made it work," Dirk said truthfully.

In 2020 most people in Salford spent most of their time being locked up at home. At some points they were allowed out for exercise, such as a walk in the park. They were intrigued when they saw what Dirk was doing.

"We were in the open air," Dirk explained. "You didn't need masks. We were one of the few places in central Salford where you could drop in and meet people and have a chat. The tea, the allotments, were a bonus."

Dirk had no trouble in signing people up to take over the old raised beds. It was a hobby, a pastime, an adventure.

"It's all very impressive," Mr Corsh said, as if he had bothered to see it all and walk his way round. In fact, his assistant had done the research, as usual. Cyril had seen some photos, plus short bursts of video. That was enough.

"Now," Mr Corsh went on, "I'd like to hear more, such as your plans for the future."

Dirk Forrest was torn.

He was proud of what he had achieved and what his regular attenders had built, over the year, but he was loath to share all his dreams with this intruding businessman. Deep in his gut, he knew that anyone call Corsh couldn't be trusted.

On the other hand, rich benefactors were exactly what he needed right now. Would the Corsh Corporation be willing to sponsor any of the development plans? Why not? To them the sums required were peanuts.

Dirk started: "I want solar panels on the Pavilion roof."

That wasn't as easy as it sounded. The Pavilion was like a square with the corners cut off. It made the task of installing solar panels a bit of a jigsaw puzzle. There were too many sharp edges. It could be done, he supposed, but -

He went on: "There's a container on the side of the Pavilion. A shipping container. It holds all the gardening tools. I'd like to put another container on top, moored at an angle, with windows, then get access from inside the Pavilion, up stairs and out through the roof. It would make an amazing Cafe, with great views, down through the trees to the road."

Mr Corsh gasped at that. Impressive, he was thinking. Yes, that would be a unique experience.

Dirk said: "These chairs and tables are a nuisance. We have to put them out, then take them back in again, every day. My idea is to build some cages on the side of the Pavilion, and lock them all in there at night. They're metal!"

Sure, aluminium, Cyril was thinking. No rust. Hey, this guy is smart! I like him.

"More ideas?" he prompted, and Dirk looked conspiratorial. Sure, there was a lot more.

"We need a greenhouse," he said. "Maybe we could have a wooden one, a smaller version of the one up behind the Manor House. Plus a polytunnel, for growing seeds. Then, maybe a straw bale building, on the other side of the Croquet lawn. There used to be a second Pavilion over there. We could reinstate it, with more solar panels, of course."

"If you had the money, enough money," Cyril suggested, "you could have a chairlift up to here from the lower road. Some of these old folks have to struggle to get up the slope. You game for that?"

Dirk stared. Wow, that was one thing he had never thought of! Hey, this guy was wild.

He felt a little closer to the moneyed man, so he shared a small privacy.

"If we're going to survive down here," he confided to Cyril, "we're going to have to see off The Friends of the Manor House. They're going in completely the wrong direction. There's bound to come a time we really clash."

Cyril sat back, looking pleased with himself. He looked at Dirk. This is the horse I'm betting on, he decided.

He said: "I wouldn't worry about Marilyn, my friend. I've bought her off, with the offer of a job."

Dirk Forrest had no idea what that meant, but he was willing to accept the assertion. It sounded helpful.

Cyril said: "Now it's my turn, and I'll tell you what I want."

Dirk nodded. Fair enough.

"What I want first is Lunch," the rich man said. "Would you care to accompany me? My bus is parked on the road."

Again, Dirk was lost, but Cyril pushed back his chair, stood up and led them downhill.

"You've only got biscuits," Cyril explained, "so I had to bring my own chef. I hope you're not insulted."

Dirk nodded. He rarely ate lunch. This sounded intriguing.

Mr Corsh wasn't going to waste a short walk by stopping talking, so he went right on ahead.

"Our company are property developers," he told Dirk, as they strolled down the path. "My plan would be to develop the Manor House. We've got our own team - we could do it at cost. If Salford City Council gave me two million, it would cover the structural work. All I'm asking is the chance to develop the old Depot area into a brand new Garden Centre. We've got several in Greater Manchester. We have the experience, the skills and the budget."

Dirk was listening. If there was one thing he'd like to see it was a Garden Centre. His dream was that his growing area could supply seedlings and small plants for sale, and the veg and fruit they grew could go to a Cafe.

They reached the bus. It was a double-decker bus, a real bus, but it had been converted into a mobile restaurant. Maybe the Corsh company used it around their building sites, Dirk was thinking. Then, when he got inside, he had second thoughts. This was far too grand for builders. It was Executive standard, at least.

Marilyn was already there.

She seemed strangely reticent. Because she had been 'bought off' by Corsh? Whatever reason, she greeted Dirk and there was no hint of animosity. They were all good friends, when everyone was a guest of the Corsh empire.

Cyril gave instructions for the chefs on the top deck to start serving food and it arrived in small and delicate portions. It reminded Marilyn of her first dinner with Cyril Corsh. It was exquisite. I like living like this, she was thinking.

There was a large table on the lower deck of the bus, with many chairs. As Marilyn and Dirk ate, the place gradually filled up. Men in suits, mainly. Mr Corsh greeted them warmly and gave introductions.

"My team," he said proudly. "Architects. Lawyers. Accountants. Garden Designers. I hope that soon, in the near future, we will all be working together at our joint project here. Are you with me, people? I want you all on board!"

Perhaps it was the glass of wine, but even Dirk felt willing to listen and share. Marilyn concurred too.

Then the police arrived.

Cyril Corsh welcomed them all in, introducing them too. Fraud Squad. Tax Inspectors. They were all welcome.

"You're soon going to be witnessing history being made here, in Salford," he said grandly. "I'm persuading the City Council to let me have the land on the old Agecroft Colliery site. They say you can't build skyscrapers on old mine workings, but I'm going to prove them wrong. I want to build a Corsh Curtain Hotel, two towers, with a wall of bedrooms in between, coming down from each tower, like a hanging curtain. It will be spectacular."

"You're building on top of the old mine?" Dirk asked, marvelling. "Aren't you afraid of subsidence?"

"The Corsh Curtain will be a copy of a hotel I've already built in the Persian Gulf," Cyril said, laughing, "and there, it's built on sand! Don't worry, Mr Forrest. No little pigs - no offence, police guys - are going to blow it down."

Cyril Corsh wanted to seal their new friendship. He called for champagne, and the glasses were passed around.

"Remember one thing," he said, as he led a toast for the Corsh Corporation, "they call me Midas. How can I fail?"

Chapter Nineteen: Old Bones

The next day Caulfield met Mr Smithers in Irlam and they had a talk. It was lunchtime.

Richard Caulfield wasn't sure how the message had come. Firstly, he'd had an early morning call from Terry, giving him a location in Port Salford to check out. It seemed routine, all part of the ongoing investigation, but what he'd witnessed there was shattering and he felt the hammer blows of trauma. He was pleased, therefore, when he got a simple text which read: 'Irlam Station'. Maybe it was telling him he could meet with Terry there, he reasoned, and would be able to share.

Instead, he found the mysterious Smithers, tucking into a delicious Starter.

"Come join me," Smithers said happily. "The Menu is delightful."

Caulfield stood by a chair, looking down at the weirdly dressed man with the bow tie.

"I haven't got a Warrant," he said cautiously. "I can't force you to tell me anything."

"Ah, you want information," Smithers muttered, between mouthfuls. "That's no problem. Sit. Eat."

Caulfield found himself slumping into the chair, with the breath going out of him. He felt defeated.

"I need help," he confessed, unable to carry on the pretence of a capable, forceful man.

Smithers smiled, but didn't stop to talk before he had cleared his plate.

He said: "This Bistro/Bar is amazing. Who knew an old railway station could be converted into such a gem? And look - the trains are still running through. I love what they've done to the old place. The rafters are still intact. Great wood."

Caulfield was still looking at the large laminated Menu in his hands. The words were swimming in front of him.

A little lady came round with a notepad. She waited expectantly. Caulfield continued to dither.

"I'll have the lamb for Mains," Smithers told her happily. "The Starter was wonderful."

"And this gentleman?"

"He's having the same as I am. Start him on the avocado but bring out the Main Course whenever it's ready. He can catch up," Smithers said, and passed his small plate over for taking away.

The waitress swept it up with a flourish. It was all very efficient. She didn't harass them at all.

Smithers said: "I'm sure there's no one within earshot. There's people in the corner, and sound behind the staircase, but if we keep our voices down - You want a story, right? You want to know how dirty he is."

Caulfield put down the Menu, glad he didn't need it anymore, but he looked at Smithers with interest.

This man was thinking the main topic of conversation was going to be his boss, Mr Cyril Corsh?

There were other things troubling Caulfield. It wasn't all about the American.

Smithers said, quietly: "He's not American. He was born in Bolton, moved to Boston in Lincolnshire. and maybe that gave him the idea of moving to the USA. He went to Harvard to finish his MA, then did an MBA there too."

An academic? Caulfield was baffled. Then when did the guy turn to crime?

"Cyril Corsh is a part, a distant part, of a huge commercial empire," Smithers said, sipping water. "His elders and betters in Manchester were happy to give such a highly qualified scion some business to do for them."

"In New York?"

"In Chicago. The market is much more open there. Less secretive. He fitted right in."

Mr Caulfield's first plate of food arrived. He looked at it doubtfully. He had been feeling sick for the last hour.

"We'll have some wine," Smithers said decisively. "Red, I think, to go with the lamb, but not too heavy."

The man in the glasses ignored Caulfield's hesitancy, and carried on speaking - once the waiter had gone.

"Cyril Corsh, the innocent new kid on the block," Smithers said, "was given the responsibility of building the new Corsh Hotel on the shores of Lake Michigan. It was a mighty tower, reaching to the sky. Great views."

How could that have possibly been a problem, Caulfield wondered?

"Such an edifice is mainly concrete. Who do you think controls the cement in Chicago?"

The waiter, the man, came back with a bottle of wine and went through the ritual of pouring some for Smithers to try. He sipped decorously, then waved a limp hand and told him to leave the bottle. They would help themselves.

"The Mob," Smithers said. "You can't avoid them. They do you 'a favour' and you have to do something in return. The first move wasn't so bad. Mr Corsh was told to buy a boatload of cars and send them out on the lake, headed for the St Lawrence Seaway and Europe. The ship mysteriously sunk. For the insurance, as you might suspect."

He poured wine for Caulfield, not caring whether the smartly dressed investigator drank it or not. He took off his glasses, polished them on his tie and drank a full half glass in one go. He needed it, he was thinking.

"I drink," Mr Smithers said informatively, "not because I like the taste, but because it is my companion."

You're lonely? Caulfield suddenly thought, but didn't say anything out loud.

"Where did you meet?" he asked, and Smithers seemed pleased to answer the question.

"He picked me up in Boston," he said, "and we've been travelling together ever since."

Boston UK or Boston USA? Caulfield wondered. This wasn't making a lot of sense to his befuddled brain.

Smithers went on: "The next job was worse. There was an old section of the Stock Yards that the Mob wanted to develop for housing. They knew they wouldn't get permission for themselves, so they used Mr Corsh as a front."

"Didn't that work?"

"People died."

Smithers poured more wine, really getting into the bottle. Caulfield sat silently, reaching for the right words.

"He killed them?" he asked at last.

"Not at all!" Smithers protested. "But he stood by and watched it happen. That's when his hands got dirty."

He was a witness, Caulfield was thinking, as are we all.

His day had started early, with a phone call from Terry. The technician was excited. His tracker had 'come alive', he said. Poor Mr Caulfield needed more of a story, and Terry told him that the tracking device that he had installed on the coffins in the Manor House cellar had started working again. It had seemed like it was dead, but now it was alive.

"These things happen," Terry burbled. "They're small, tiny batteries. They fade, they burst into life. What can I say?"

What he did say was a postcode and an address. He wanted Caulfield to get down there and investigate.

Strictly speaking, the Deputy Director could plan his own agenda for the day, but this was an interesting one. It all linked up to the stash of drugs, and that led to Caulfield's neighbours, so he felt as though he had skin in the game.

He dressed, impressively, as always, took his time and made porridge, then set off in his car, heading west.

The first leg of the journey was easy. The co-ordinates took him directly to Port Salford, on the banks of the River Irwell.

He had to flash his ID, but that worked spectacularly. The cowed young man in t-shirt and yachting cap, seemed physically scared. The slogan on his chest said, 'Live for Today', but he acted like he thought that was all he had.

They were standing on the quay and Caulfield was pointing his phone in front of him. It was beeping, from the app that Terry had sent him. It was pointing directly at a stack of shipping containers that were being loaded by crane onto a waiting ship. The process was proceeding, and the young man thought there was nothing that could stop it.

"I need to look at that container there," Caulfield said. "Tell the crane driver to lower it down."

"You can't stop the loading!" the kid said desperately. "Okay, look, you're pointing at that one, right? I know what's in it. We searched it before it went up, but my boss had been given a little incentive already and we had to let it go."

Money? A bribe? A kickback, Caulfield was thinking? That already makes it dirty.

"Tell me what you found," he demanded.

"Empty boxes," the young man said, squirming a little. "But expensive caskets, the sort that sell well in America. Still, the dog was going wild. There was traces of drugs there, but nothing else. The coffins might have contained bodies, but they weren't there. They might have had expensive silk linings, but that had all been stripped out, back to the wood - "

Caulfield stared. Somebody had done this, but not this dockside worker in front of him. This young man had simply been told to ignore the suspiciously smelling coffins and make sure the container they were in was loaded immediately.

If Mr Caulfield insisted on searching the container for himself, it was going to screw up the loading schedule and might even delay the departure of the ship. That was his biggest concern.

At this point, fairly early in the day, Caulfield was capable of sustained thought.

So, I know where the coffins have ended up, he was thinking. This is the last stage of the journey. They're going abroad and will be sold for a profit. Not much to complain about there.

Then - the drugs. Well, they had been taken out and Caulfield knew where they went - down his alley, so to speak. A little close to home. That had all been explained too, and though that gave him a dilemma - was he going to turn in his neighbours or not - he didn't need any more information. He had seen the evidence with his own eyes.

No, the only missing link in the whole chain was the question of the corpses and what happened to them.

That's when Terry gave him the second call of the day. New information and it made Caulfield thank the young man, and then, much to the kid's relief, leave. There was another place to check out in Irlam.

In some ways, it was exactly as Caulfield had always thought. The answer was in the old deserted steel mill.

The ruins were back from the river, nearer the main road. Once, back in the 1980s maybe, the whole area had been prosperous and booming, thanks to the one major industry. But the economy suffered a series of massive shocks, mainly thanks to overseas rivals, and new imports were cheaper and more readily available. The steel industry wasn't the only one to suffer, but it was one of the most visible. The closure of steel mills hollowed out whole communities, not just in the North West.

Much of the ground that the old mill covered had been cleared, as Caulfield knew. There were new units on top of the old land now, mainly distribution warehouses and small industrial units. But the parts of Irlam that backed directly onto the new supermarket was a landlocked enclave, waiting for a new access road to be built. Caulfield could walk to it from where he was, so he did, hiking across a field and through a bit of scrub land and woods. It wasn't far.

Caulfield clambered over a low fence and came into a paved area. This had once been part of the loading bays. There was a big shed to his right - and fresh tyre tracks. How had they - maybe an SUV crossing the muddy field.

He walked in through the high open door and came into a mass of tangled metal and empty cauldrons. Over in one corner, a pile of metal shavings was slowly smoking. Recent fires. He got closer. The smell got worse.

It was dark in the shed, but he had brought a flash-light and clicked it on. He waved it across the floor.

White sticks? There were piles of white dust and sticks poking out of the piles. It looked like -

Bones. They were bones. Human, no doubt. Here were the remains of the people in the coffins, right down to the last General, and all the ranks in between. Apart from the one survivor, pulled out on the night. The rest -

"Mr Caulfield," Smithers said, pulling him back to the present. "Are you gay?"

Caulfield told him he wasn't.

"Then you can't possibly know the agony of unrequited love." Smithers sighed. "But you must know one thing - I shall never betray Cyril Corsh, no matter how badly he treats me. I wouldn't. But of course I don't need to."

"Why is that?" Caulfield asked, scanning the other man's face for an expression of emotion.

"Because he will destroy himself. Just you see. It's only a matter of time."

Chapter Twenty: Fun

Marilyn organised a Barbecue, directly outside the Manor House.

It was a 'Welcome' event for the Funfair, that sprawled over the lawns in front of her usual working area. Most people, she told her little team, were dismissive of these travelling folk, but Fair people had a rich and interesting history. They were a separate sub-culture that was worthy of study. If we wanted to be inclusive, she said -

It was worse than that, of course. Most people in Salford didn't really trust these travellers. They felt that they would be trying to part them from their money while they were in town, by any means at hand. They were happy to come along to the park and enjoy the rides, but then they would go home and lock their doors, fearing the visitors.

It was a cold and crisp autumn evening. Melia had put on a warm winter coat, for a change, and was working her way along the line of caravans near the road, where the Fair folk lived and slept.

She had been given a tip-off.

Someone from Marilyn's team told her that she had seen someone answering Emma's description. A young girl, she said? Yes, she saw her one morning while walking her dog. The youngster was happily helping the Fair set up.

Melia was unhappy with the news, but mightily relieved. She hadn't seen her niece since that night she disappeared, and the sighting was a possible solution to the mystery of where she had gone. It was also a reversal of what the little people, the elves and fairies, had told her. They said Emma feared the Fair and had fled. The new information seemed to be the opposite - Emma had joined the circus, willingly. If so, Melia wouldn't worry. The youngster was free to do whatever she liked with her life, but Melia needed to know. She was her Godmother. She needed to be reassured Emma was all right.

With loud music playing in the background, and the joyous screams of people on board the dangerous rides, Melia knocked on the next door of the mobile homes. It was frustrating. So far she had encountered a tight-lipped and closed community, not wanting to share information. Who did they think she was? The police?

Maybe it really was a clash of cultures, she was thinking. These people had a history of keeping to themselves, not risking interaction with the wider life of society. Their natural reaction was to clam up, say nothing. That was what they did.

The next caravan solved that dilemma.

Emma answered the door.

"I love him, Auntie Mel," Emma said, after she had invited her in and made her a cup of tea.

Melia felt used. Emma had arrived on her doorstep because she knew she would get a warm welcome, and it was a place to stay while waiting for the Fair to arrive in town. Then she decamped to live with the young man.

"Where is he now?" she asked Emma. Melia would like to meet whoever had stolen her niece's heart.

"He works on the Waltzer," she was told.

So, it was an old tale. The Fair spent time in Emma's town. She had visited one night, several nights, and met a mysterious and good-looking stranger. When the business packed up and started to leave, Emma wanted to go with them.

He resisted at first, assuring Emma that what she felt was simply an infatuation. Emma sought to contradict that impression. She found out where the Fair was going next and followed them. She turned up on his doorstep.

He was impressed by her determination, and allowed her in.

Then they left town again.

"Emma," Melia said gently, "maybe he doesn't want it to be serious. Maybe he has other loves."

The youngster looked whimsical. "He loves the life of the open road, but that's why I love him."

Melia, barely thirty herself, found it interesting that she was handing out life advice to someone roughly half her age.

Maybe I should let her get on with it, she was thinking, but that thought upset her. I have a responsibility, she concluded. Because of what had happened, with her sister, all those years ago. The wound hadn't healed.

She had tried phoning, and the conversation was stilted and short. Melia had asked if they knew where Emma had gone, and what her intentions were and Melia's sister had closed off that line of enquiry.

"It's her life," she said. "She's making her own choices."

As always, her sister irritated the hell out of her.

"Don't you care?" Melia snapped.

"About as much as you, Auntie Mel," was the sarcastic reply. "Why don't you leave us alone, like you usually do?"

"Emma," Melia said, looking at her God-daughter across the table, "I'm going to the Manor House's barbecue. Why don't you come and join us? You're very welcome, all the Fair people are. Marilyn wants to meet you all."

"Maybe later," Emma said tightly, as if she knew it was what Melia wanted to hear.

Melia passed her a card. It included her business details.

"There's my number there," she said, "and the office number. Ring me any time, day or night. If I don't reply, they will find me. And - well, if you need a place to stay, then turn up at my flat. You're welcome, any time."

Emma smiled and gave her Auntie a hug.

"I think I'll be all right," she said, but her voice had a little wobble. She was so young!

* * * * *

Marilyn had applied for a grant, which paid for the night's activities.

It was Arts-based, which meant she had commissioned musicians to play in the Kitchen Garden, and willow weavers to make a series of hearts, which hung from the railings. There was bunting and some paintings too.

But the centre piece of her efforts was going to be the Wicker Man, and the Fair folk were making it for her.

Her team joked that Lord Turnton could be the sacrifice that they put inside it, before setting it on fire, but nobody meant that seriously. They hadn't seen the alleged 'owner' of the Manor House recently, so it was hard to maintain a grudge against someone you didn't see. Maybe he moved on, people said, (hoping it was true).

Marilyn played up to the suggestions. She was happy people were turning against the usurper - Turnton. It would make them more willing to accept the newcomer, Cyril Corsh. If there was going to be a competition over the future of the Manor House, then, Marilyn had decided, she wanted Mr Corsh to win. He had the finances - both to make the refurb at Buile Hill stack up, but then follow it up with a new career for Marilyn. That was what really thrilled her.

Still, she was serious about the Barbecue. She wanted that to be a success. She had planned it, launched it. She wanted as many people as possible to be there. It was like a 'project' for her. She wanted to proved she had the capability to get things done. Then the rich man wouldn't regret making her a job offer, she thought.

It was getting on towards eleven o'clock and the younger kids had drifted off home, maybe meeting a parental curfew. The Fair people, sensing a terminal decline in trade, started shutting down their rides and stalls, one by one, and walked up to take a seat around the fire. They had a surprise for Marilyn. They brought fireworks.

Well, we're supplying the fire and food, she was thinking. Why not let them make a contribution?

Rockets started roaring into the air. Whizz bangs, flashes, and screechers filled the silence now that many of the rides had turned off their annoying, grating pop music. It was like a real Bonfire Night, which would have been happening around this time of year, if not for Covid. The City Council had cancelled their official firework display at short notice, quoting medical concerns. It made more trade for the Fair, since people still wanted to go out, and more longing for a few large fireworks, bigger than the tiny things that were sold for backyard consumption.

The Fair people brought professional size flashers, and filled the night sky, blocking out the New Moon.

Melia picked up a vegan burger from one of the barbecues - it was all free - and settled in a seat.

Looking around, she was surprised to see Emma sitting nearby. The girl had arms linked with a young man.

"You gonna introduce me?" she asked, walking cautiously nearer.

Emma was proud of her catch.

"This is Rummy," she said, a huge smile showing on her face in the glow from the fire.

"Rumi," the young man said. "After the Persian poet."

Melia nodded. She had travelled enough in the Gulf to know that name. Famous in many Middle Eastern countries.

"Please sit down," the young man said politely. "Em's told me about you. Now's your chance."

He had slicked back black hair. He was wearing a leather jacket over a sloganned t-shirt.

Also, he had his right arm in a sling.

He could 'work the Waltzer' with that?

"I won't shake hands," Melia muttered. "You've had a recent accident?"

The young man flashed bright teeth at Emma. His experience wasn't a secret.

"I got shot," he told Melia. "I went over the fence into the Depot and came face-to-face with an armed man."

He grinned at Emma, as though he was merely the victim of an everyday occurrence.

"You went over the fence?" Melia said, knowing she had done the same. But - a man with a gun? An armed guard?

"I was looking for scrap metal," Rumi said. "It's what we do. We tend to live on what the rest of the world throws away. It's no big deal. I've been chased off sites with dogs and men with shotguns before. But not a man in uniform."

This isn't a shotgun wound, Melia could see. This was caused by a handgun. A police or Security Service issue. Or Army.

Melia had more questions. Just like mothers, parents, and Aunts everywhere, her stance with Emma would be to say, 'You're associating with a boy who can get himself into this sort of trouble? What exactly do you know about him?'

Before she had the chance to go further, there was the clear sound of screaming from the Manor House.

Marilyn and some of her helpers stood up at once, and started to move, as if they could guess what was going on.

Melia followed, keen to see what all the fuss was about.

It was Suze.

She had a flash-light in her hand and had levelled it on the face of a new visitor. Dirk Forrest.

"I told you never to come back!" she howled. "You've ruined my life once. You want a second chance?"

"It's not about you," he told her evenly. "Your fireworks are landing on my planting beds. Flowers are dying."

Apart from the question of what he was doing down the slope in the middle of the night, Melia had the question of what did he expect when fireworks were around? Rockets went up, they came down. It was unfortunate.

"Please stop shouting," a voice beside her said. "You're disturbing the dogs."

It was Rumi. He was standing with a clutch of his compatriots from the Fair community. Men. They all seemed to have the most growly dogs Melia had ever seen. All on chains. So far.

She wanted to laugh. These dogs hadn't twitched a hair when the fireworks exploded, but were now turning into nervous wrecks to hear a woman go loudly off her rocker? Were they serious?

During the next half an hour, she found out.

By then, she was back in a seat, around the quietly glowing bonfire, close to Emma and Rumi.

Suze, the screamer, found it impossible to control herself and one of Rumi's friends had found it impossible to control his hound. The brute slipped his chain and leapt upon the poor unfortunate woman. Other Fair folk tried to intervene, but only succeeded in allowing their beasts to get close to the action. The dogs were acting as a pack, taking turns to bite great chunks out of Suze. By the time the ambulance arrived, she was covered in blood, rolling on the ground.

"We're taking her to hospital," one of the paramedics announced.

"Best place for her," one of Marilyn's trusted companions said bitterly. There was no sympathy there.

Strangely, Dirk offered to go with her, but when he took a step up into the ambulance, she managed a dull whimper, making it clear he was the last person on Earth she wanted for comfort and moral support.

Instead, Marilyn took him off to dance, on the lawn behind the Conference Rooms. They whirled around the spotlighted grass, moving to tunes she played on her phone. It was Old Style, ballroom stuff.

As if from nowhere, dressed up imps and elves came to surround them, adding to the Fairy Tale vibe.

Melia, on the other hand, was delighted when Fair folk arrived with fiddles, mandolins and Irish drums. They started playing some of the old Ceilidh music she loved so much. She was delighted to see

Emma join in the country dances, even bringing in Rumi. He couldn't link hands with that arm in a sling, but she steered him by his shoulder.

In the bonfire light, under a half moon and bright starlight, Melia had to admit she hadn't had so much fun in ages.

Chapter Twenty One: Folk Tale

"Your children haven't been attending school," the official-looking woman told the older woman at her own front door.

It was the Woodcutter's wife. They were standing outside her humble cottage. She invited them in.

There were three of them. Two from Education Support Services in Salford, and a policeman. His name was Sergeant Don Fellowes. He didn't want to be there. His usual beat was Murder, Homicide and Grand Theft, but his new boss didn't like him and was giving him all the mundane jobs. Accompany the Truancy Officers for the day?

"You will do exactly what I say, Mr Fellowes," the Inspector said, "and then maybe you will learn some real policing. At the very least, you will learn how to follow orders and get results."

The 'results' that the new boss had in mind was finding the new drug pushers in Seedley and Langworthy. There was a tsunami of fresh drugs fuelling the area and the cops had no leads. Don Fellowes, despite his best efforts, had come up with nothing. That's why he had appealed to Melia, but there was no result there. That's why he was now baby-sitting the School Attendance duo in their unwelcome job of harassing recalcitrant parents.

At least the house was interesting, Don was thinking.

It was at the far end of Buile Hill, the east end of Seedley Park side, and had obviously been a Park Keeper's house, when the City had such things. More than a few years ago now, the Local Authority had been forced to make cuts, and resident people who looked after the parks were swept away in favour of a smaller, more mobile team of Rangers.

The Park Rangers had a lot of ground to cover, which was one reason why there was no one there to defend the Depot in Buile Hill when the vandals came to attack the buildings and smash windows. It was the reason that the Manor House had first been abandoned to any productive use, but then had to be boarded up. No money, so cuts to services. Cuts Cuts, Cuts.

That was the explanation for why no one had bothered the Woodcutter and his wife, up to now. Weeks had gone by and the school had noticed that their children were missing school, but the Support Team that went out and visited homes, trying to find answers, had been decimated. The pair here, the ones that Don was looking after for the day, were not the only ones left - on paper - but the others were mostly off sick because of the pressure, or were resigning in frustration.

Don sighed. It was an awful job, unappreciated and badly rewarded. They were trying, he was thinking. They had the interests of the children at heart. They wanted the kids of Salford to get the best education possible. But -

Well, like now. They were invited in by the Woodcutter's wife, only to reveal that the cottage was a complete mess. Nobody had tidied or cleaned recently, it was obvious. The wife sat down at the table, where she had been idly looking at a magazine, and looked untidy herself, uncared for and barely coping. The visitors felt sorry for her.

"Where is your husband?" the woman said. "We'd like to talk to you both."

The wife looked around, as if considering this a difficult question and she was searching for answers.

"Oh, it's afternoon," she said. "He will be in the pub."

The man and the woman looked at each other and exchanged a disapproving look.

"And the children," the man said, doing his job. "Where are your children?"

"Off out," she said vaguely. "In the woods. The woods of old Buile Hill."

She looked scared, as well she might. She didn't want to have to tell the full story to these officials, with their smart uniforms and clipboards. The children? They had been taken into the wood by their father, weeks ago. and had only been back for the briefest of visits since, none of which had lasted long. Despite the couple thinking that they had come to an arrangement with the Magus, the magical man of the forest, the kids seemed determined to forget their biological parents and go and live with him. One rescue mission after another had failed miserably.

It had got to the point where the adults couldn't discuss, especially her. Since her husband hardly talked to her at all any more, and when he did speak he didn't actually tell her anything about anything, she had no idea where they were, how they were, or what they were doing. She was completely in the dark, suffering. Also, poor, with no prospect of money coming in. Her husband kept telling her about grand schemes and dreams of prosperity, but she had seen none of it.

"She's depressed," Don hissed at the Truancy Team. "You'll get nothing out of her today."

The woman inspector looked sour.

"This family has been on the list for ages," she reminded the policeman. "If we leave now, we won't be coming back."

Don nodded, aware of the dire situation in their office.

The detective in him was stirred, however. No sign of the husband? A wife who had completely sunk into despair? What was really going on? If he had still been working at his usual level of authority, he would have insisted on going to this 'pub' that had been mentioned, to find the husband and demand answers.

* * * * *

Such a plan might have worked.

The Woodcutter, at that precise moment, was indeed 'sitting in the pub'. He too was 'in despair', but it wasn't just his poverty or his failures as a drug dealer or a parent. There was more for him to worry about. A lot more.

The trees were dying.

A beetle, a tiny insect, had entered the country illegally and was sweeping up from the South East at an alarming rate. The larvae were being planted under the bark and were eating away at the heart of the trees and slowly killing them.

He'd seen infections before. But that had been limited to single species, like Dutch Elm Disease or Ash Die-back. This was nothing he had ever seen in his adult life, working as a woodcutter and tree conservator. It was a huge worry, and it kept him up at night. No trees meant no cutting. Oh, sure, he had the skeletons of fallen trees to attend to, but the Council's rules were that any victims of the disease had to be burnt and securely disposed. They didn't allow him to ply his trade and sell logs anymore. He had been cut off at the roots.

It was afternoon, and a weekday at that, but not too busy. He would have survived, but then the students arrived.

It wasn't far from Salford University, as the crow flies, and an increasing number of the kids were living nearby, in converted terraced houses. Landlords were finding it a lucrative trade, and encouraged it. After all, the only young people who went to Tertiary Education these days were the children of the rich, so they had lots of money to spend on rent.

And drinks.

It looked like they had had a busy morning, and were now relaxing, perhaps with something to celebrate. There were about six of them and half were carrying banners. They'd been on a picket, maybe. A demo?

"What's your sign say?" he asked a girl when she sat down near him.

It read 'Organics or Die'. A bit dramatic, he thought, although, strictly speaking, it was entirely accurate.

A boy sat down. His t-shirt read: 'No more chemicals on the land'. The woodcutter smiled at the irony.

He said: "I could do with some chemicals right now. I need to kill the beetles that are killing my trees."

The demonstrators didn't seem to see the humour in that at all. They rounded on him, aggressively.

"We need to phase out the use of pesticides, right now," the boy declared, as if it was a manifesto pledge.

The Woodcutter said: "Yes, but if you knew what I know about larvae - "

"There's no excuse for interfering in the order of Mother Nature," the girl said, simplifying things.

"I agree with you," the woodsman said, "about this most of the time. But Nature can throw you a curve ball - "

"Wait a minute," another one of the lads said quietly. "Shut up, you two. I know this man. Don't I?"

The Woodcutter looked at the lanky kid. Long hair, dirty. Could be anybody, he was thinking.

"No, No," the kid went on, but keeping his voice down. "You're the man with the drugs, aren't you?"

Their whole attitude changed. Suddenly, he was an ally. A helper. A supplier.

"I've got nothing right now," the older man told them sadly.

He didn't go into his sad story, how he had been cheated and robbed. How his life had started to collapse.

The students seemed disgusted enough with him already. They perceived him as a betrayer of the natural order, for wanting to put chemicals onto naturally growing things. As for their own needs, they wanted him to supply them with chemicals they put in their own bodies to make themselves more cheerful, more wide-eyed and able to cope with their hectic social lives.

They might have simply ignored him, knowing he was no longer any use to them, but then the Woodcutter did the strangest thing. He leapt to his feet, knocking his chair over onto the floor and rushed towards the bar.

A man was standing there, a man who had just come in. But not just any man. He was The Man.

The Woodcutter was strong and tall. He pinned the Man to the bar and reached for his throat.

"You cheated me!" he hissed, with an anger he rarely felt.

This was The Man, the one who had supplied him with pills and taken his money. But the pills were fake.

"Take it easy," the drug dealer said. "We've all been cheated. The children made me do it to you."

The Woodcutter dropped his fist, lost for words. They were talking about - Was he saying -

"The kids who live above the Conference Suite," the Man said, breathing heavy. "You must know them."

'Know them'? That contingent included his own two offspring, the Woodcutter was thinking.

"Tell me more," he said.

The Man shook his head, as if he wanted to wave some reality into it. "I don't know much."

The Woodcutter raised his fist again, as if he was considering knocking the truth out of him.

"They control all of the drugs around here now," the Man said sadly. "We are all following orders."

"I gave you money!" the Woodcutter said.

"And I gave it to them."

The woodsman considered. Slowly, painstakingly, he realised he had little choice left in his life anymore.

"You're coming with me," he told the Man. "We're going to get our money back. All of it."

The Man was a drug seller not a fighter, but maybe he thought he might have a chance with this big, tall lumberjack at his side. Besides, the big man seemed to have some sort of little hatchet in his belt. He was armed.

The pair of ill-assorted and unsuccessful businessmen walked out of the pub, across the road and towards the gate of old Buile Hill. They entered the Seedley side gate and climbed the slope. The Man wasn't as fit as he looked, and was panting by the time they reached the Conference Rooms. He was thinking furiously, trying to come up with a plan.

The Woodcutter was way ahead of him. He started shouting.

"Come out! Come out you little devils!" he bellowed. "Don't hide in there. Don't make me come in and get you!"

A little boy, maybe ten years old, appeared around the corner. He was dressed all in green, like an elf.

"More!" the woodsman yelled. "Bring out more of them! They need to explain themselves, whoever is in charge."

"There's no one in charge," the elf commented, but he blew a whistle anyway, and his companions emerged.

The two men were now surrounded by a dozen pre-pubescent youngsters, not one in normal clothes. There were elves, gnomes and fairy folk. They didn't need introductions. They knew full well who the adults were.

"Where's the Magus?" the Woodcutter demanded angrily.

"We got rid of him ages ago," one kid said. "We make our own way now. We rule each other."

The Man, the drug dealer, didn't seem at all surprised, but the Woodcutter gaped, both at him and at the children.

The Man took instruction from these little kids? What kind of topsy-turvy world was it?

"You'd better believe him, Dad," a familiar voice said.

The Woodcutter turned, and was confronted by his own son. The boy's sister stood four-square beside him.

A few minutes later and the Woodsman was sunk in a heap beside the Conference Centre. The Man had fled, as soon as his 'protector' dissolved in tears. Most of the tiny people had turned and gone back up the stairs to their quarters.

Only a young boy and girl were left, looking at their father pityingly.

"We aren't coming home," they said again, just to be sure the message had got through.

"Here," the boy said. "We're making good money now and we can look after you and Mum."

He stuffed a wad of bills into the top pocket of the Woodcutter's heavy jacket.

The woodsman howled.

It was the final humiliation.

Chapter Twenty Two: Drowning, slowly

Dirk was on his way to work when he saw the baby in the sump pond.

He leapt over the fence at once, without thinking, and plunged into the water.

It was a doll, a small plastic doll, but around the size of a new born babe, so easily mistaken.

It's a warning, Dirk Forrest thought to himself. Somebody is trying to tell me something.

The most obvious message was that after a full night of torrential rain, the ground was sodden and the pond was full. The sun was shining now, but it was cold. The autumn is turning into winter, he was thinking.

Dirk had come into the park from the Eccles gate. He had walked from the hospital. It had only been a check-up, but he wasn't going to talk to anybody about what happened. That was tempting Fate, he reckoned. He didn't want to be ill.

He walked up the path at the back of the croquet lawn. It was a slight slope and he could see through the railings and brambles that the green was shining healthily but not wet. Good drainage there, he noted.

Coming round the corner and down into the Seedley south side of old Buile Hill, he came across the new lake.

Marilyn was standing by the steps, looking down. She had old photographs in her hands.

"This is where the lake used to be," she said wisely, and showed Dirk the pictures.

Dirk knew that Seedley Park, as it once was, had a small lake, plus other features, like a bandstand. It was all in the ancient photos, but the present view was different, and had been since the Second World War.

Dirk looked down. The thicket of trees nearby, which was a useful haunt of homeless people, who threw their sleeping bags down amongst the bushes and were glad to be shielded from the sight of casual passers-by, was now an island.

The 'lake' stretched almost to the southern gate, on Lower Seedley Road. The ground must already have been wet, Dirk was thinking, after a week of steady downpours, but last night it must have got a real drenching.

Marilyn was strangely friendly.

Perhaps it was the historical interest she had. She didn't usually venture down to this lower part of the park - she considered it Dirk's territory - but the historical nature of the flood intrigued her and made her think.

Dirk looked at her. She wasn't a bad person, he reasoned. Since they had danced together on the night of the Funfair, he thought of her almost fondly. In some ways they had the same aims at heart - rescuing and improving the whole of Buile Hill, in all its extremities. It was just a shame that Marilyn's laser-like focus on the Manor House had sometimes twisted her vision and made her antagonistic to anyone who wasn't as committed as her.

"I'm taking pictures," Dirk declared, and pulled out his phone.

Marilyn looked at him. He's not so bad, she was thinking. It's just a pity that his absolute concentration on green and growing things sometimes blurred his oversight of the most important things that needed doing in the park.

He was tall, dark, quite attractive in some ways. She smiled at him now, happy to be in his company.

She wanted to share. Who else could she talk to? There was so much bottled up inside her.

"My team are getting militant," she said, with regret.

Some of the 'Manor House Monkeys' were planning to chain themselves to the ancient oak doors. Anything for publicity, they said. They wanted the world to know the importance of their adopted building.

There was talk of camping out in the nearby trees, the way that anti-motorway protesters did.

Marilyn shook her head. It must all seem very exciting for them, the activists, she was thinking. They hadn't been involved as long as her, seeing the ups and downs, the comings and goings. Supporters had been there, then gone. No one was that reliable. Only her, and a few valued friends, had stuck with the project over the few short, action-packed years.

Now Cyril Corsh was going to seal the deal, she was thinking. His money would make the campaign work.

She wasn't going to tell Dirk about recent news from him, the other man, she decided. Something made her want to keep the latest details from the benefactor to herself. Dirk Forrest had met Mr Corsh of course, but seemed to think of him as an amiable old eccentric, all talk and no real interest in Buile Hill. The property developer wants to build skyscrapers in Salford, Dirk concluded, and promising the world to the park project was just to earn favour.

Marilyn knew differently. She knew Cyril better than anyone else in the city. She knew he was serious.

It started to rain.

Dirk was dressed in his usual Army-style waterproof coat. Marilyn had a padded jacket on, which was shower-proof, but she had no hood. The rain poured down on her unprotected curls and her carefully coiffed hairdo started to come apart. Her mascara began to run down her face. She must look a horror, she realised.

"Come on," Dirk said decisively. "Let's get you tidied up."

He led her up the slope to his domain, opened the gate and invited her in to the Pavilion.

He switched the fan heating on and turning it up high, put the kettle on and produced towels.

"Dry yourself off," he urged. "You can stand in front of that heater. It'll be like a hair dryer."

The warm air cheered her, and the cup of tea warmed her insides. Marilyn began to recover her usual self.

"Thanks," she said quietly, realising she had never set foot in this building before, Dirk's Den.

Once the cups of tea were made he sat down, and began taking his shoes off, drying his socks as well.

"You've got wet," she noticed. He'd been paddling?

"I went swimming in the sump," he admitted, and told her about the doll.

Marilyn was horrified. She believed in signs and portents. That seemed like a very bad omen, she was thinking.

It could mean something really bad was about to happen, she was thinking.

Her mobile phone rang.

"What?" she whispered. Then, raising her voice: "What? What?"

She jumped up.

"I have to go," she told Dirk. "Trouble at the Manor House."

He knew better than to ask questions.

"There's umbrellas behind the door. Borrow one, for now, just in case. Return it next time you're here."

Next time? Marilyn was thinking. I'm coming here again, am I? You really think so, Mr Forrest?

* * * * *

By the time she got up the hill to the Manor House, Mayor Senate was introducing people to a man in a suit.

"This is Everley Bone," he told the small crowd. "He used to be a Member of Parliament. Before that he was a highly successful businessman in the world of computers. Lately, he's been turning his attention to community matters."

"Didn't you go to prison?" one of Marilyn's supporters said harshly, challenging him.

Mr Bone was suave, not easily put off. He had been a politician, after all.

"There was some unpleasantness, a misunderstanding about Parliamentary expenses. I did serve some time behind bars, but I managed to turn that disaster into a learning experience. I wrote a book about my struggle."

"What did you call it - *Mein Kampf?*" the young man snapped irritably.

"Good one," the Mayor said jocularly. He was a politician too, enjoying a good joke.

"What's on offer?" Marilyn demanded, stepping in, knowing she had to speak up for Cyril Corsh, who wasn't there.

"The best offer we've had so far," the Mayor said, grinning. "Everley is not asking for any money from the Council. He just wants the Manor House outright, and will draw up a rebuild programme before it's handed over."

"What about the Depot?" a woman asked. The usual question, The usual stalling point.

"We haven't ironed out the details," Mayor Senate said, looking to Mr Bone for confirmation.

The young man, the one who had asked a question earlier, was growing increasingly suspicious.

"You two seem awfully pally," he accused. "You know each other outside this project?"

Mr Bone seemed bashful. He smiled coquettishly, glancing at Sol Senate, the elected Mayor.

"Your Mayor and I have met socially," he admitted. "But this development plan - it's a recent conversation."

"But where?" the young man demanded. "Where did you meet? The Sacred Society? You got the secret handshake?"

"I'm Gay," Everley Bone confided. It was a secret he rarely shared readily, but this was important.

It was raining again, and all the important people had umbrellas. That included Marilyn.

But it made hearing people difficult.

"I missed that," the other woman said. She was nearest the lawn, furthest away from the Manor House.

"He's Gay," the Mayor informed her cheerfully. "But so am I - you all know that."

Was he? It hadn't been the reason everyone voted for him. But it ticked some boxes in the narrow world of local politics.

"So am I," Marilyn said, stepping forward, "and I can tell you, it isn't going to get you a free ride around here."

"So am I," a male voice said. A deep booming voice, approaching. It was Dirk.

"I've never met you 'socially'," he told Mr Bone. "But, so what? There's always a time and a place to do business."

The Mayor was defensive. "Everley's offer means a lot to the Council. It could even clear some of our debts."

"What is the offer?" another voice said, new to the scene.

It was Lord Turnton.

People turned to him in confusion. He hadn't been seen for weeks. Now here he came, traipsing in to the circle, the man who claimed title to the building, with his solicitor in tow, the woman, and another woman, (who Melia would recognise as The Housekeeper in the triangle). He was as smartly dressed as ever, and seemed happy to join in the debate.

"Don't trust this ex-MP," the young man said nastily. "He's Gay."

"So am I," Lord Turnton said, as if it wasn't a relevant fact.

"So am I," said his solicitor, wondering how she could turn the young man's denigrating tone to their advantage.

"So am I," said the Housekeeper, but nobody seemed bothered what she said. She was almost invisible.

Mr Senate, the Mayor, said, trying to clear the air: "Sexual Orientation is not relevant in this discussion. I can assure you all that it is not a deciding factor in whether the Council is going to decided to accept Everley Bone's offer."

"'Everley'?" the angry young man said. "He keeps calling him 'Everley'. You can see which side he's on!"

"Nobody has made up their minds about anything," Mayor Senate repeated.

"But why is it better than Mr Corsh's offer?" Marilyn demanded. "He owns a Property Development company. Surely that's better than Mr Bone here, with his computers and what not."

"The 'What Not', dear Lady, is Virtual Reality," Mr Bone said, smiling.

"You need the Depot for that?" she asked desperately, but nobody answered her.

This is useless, she was thinking. We're getting no answers to the most important questions.

How could they! How could the Council allow in this last-minute entrant to the race, and then promote him towards the Finish Line without even a proper public hearing! This is rigged. The whole deal is rotten!

"We will get what we're asking for," she shouted to her followers. "But we need to support Mr Corsh!"

Unfortunately, Corsh Industries had a bad reputation in this part of Salford. They had done some slick deals in their time, and never to the residents' advantage. Marilyn, her people thought, was backing the wrong horse.

Mr Bone was slipping away, allowing the Mayor to take the flak from the protesters. He looked pleased.

He practically bumped into Dirk Forrest, who looked completely underwhelmed.

"Have you got an links to Salford?" he wanted to know. "Any support from Salford, or Manchester?"

"Why, yes," Mr Bone told him, very self-satisfied. "I'm embedded with the Village Gang."

The Gay Village, in Manchester? The Gang there were some of the most vicious gangsters in the north of England!

They weren't seen very often up here at Buile Hill. They had their own territory to dominate.

Mr Bone took Dirk's hesitation for fear. He thought Dirk would be impressed by his tough friends.

"After all," Everley Bone said smoothly, "who do you think shot Al Gauze?"

Dirk Forrest scratched his memory. Al Gauze? Why he'd said it himself. He'd said -

"The Fairies, that's what he said," Mr Bone told him. "Not the little flowery characters. No. The Village Gang, that's who executed their rival, Al Gauze. The Fairies. The Fairies did it."

Chapter Twenty Three: All Bad

"I've decided to see what you've been up to," Captain Gibson was telling Melia.

He could have picked a better day, she was thinking sourly. The sun was shining and the sky was blue, but it was freezing. She was shivering, despite her woollen sweater and thick jacket. Typical, she thought. The place looked good, but you can't see the problem. The temperature doesn't show up in photographs. As long as people are smiling -

They were sitting at a table outside the Pavilion in the lower part of the park, the Seedley south side. Melia had fetched them cups of tea, which were accompanied by packets of biscuits. Melia was shocked to see that her boss picked up the pack he had been allocated, looked at it, then turned his nose up. He brought his own biscuits out of his briefcase.

"Always come prepared," he muttered, as he dunked the digestives into his tea.

"Very well," he said formally, starting the conversation. "We have walked down here, past the Manor House. You have shown me the side door where you say the coffins were delivered. You have pointed out the Conference Rooms where you say the little elves live, the ones who tried to kill you. You have shown me the front lawn where the Funfair was encamped - "

Gone now, Melia was thinking. I wish he'd seen that collection of caravans and death-defying rides, but 'the caravan has packed its tents and moved on', she was thinking, quoting Omar Khayam - or was it Rumi?.

Gibson seemed to be doing all the talking, but his speech was quiet, as if he didn't want to be overheard. There were other tables there, under the trees, and other visitors. People were coming and going all the time - dog walkers, allotment holders, volunteers and - investigators. Yes, that was the only way she could describe them.

People asking questions - young people. The University of Salford ran several undergraduate courses involving the media - such as Journalism, Mixed Media, Media Studies. Part of the students' tasks related to getting 'out into the community'. They had to find ordinary people to interview. Buile Hill had become a primary target. There was always a victim or two there - most of them, anxious to talk.

"I have to tell you," Gibson said ominously, "that Control thinks that the Russians are behind everything that is going wrong at the moment, both nationally and locally. This is based on absolutely no physical evidence, and is merely the result of chatter on the internet, and gossip on Social Media. Hardly sleuthing, as you and I would recognise it."

Melia sighed and decided to butt in. She'd heard these bizarre theories before.

"This is Salford," she told her boss. "It's a - what would you call it? - a 'lively' place. Young people here, they take every opportunity to enjoy themselves, and we're just at that time of year. We had Halloween - so, knocking on doors, dressing up as ghosts and ghouls - and then Bonfire Night, with fireworks and commemoration of Guy Fawkes."

"Yes, yes," the old man said irritably, "but aren't you finding it's a little more 'orchestrated' this year?"

Not at all, Melia was thinking. If anything, it was a bit more anarchic and disorganised than usual.

"I've talked to local Police," she said, "you know, the Community Liaison Officers. They aren't full police personnel, more like local volunteers, but they know the territory and they know the villains. They're telling me that it used to be a whole lot worse. They said that November 5th used to start in August, with fireworks every night! It's a lot less now. There are restrictions on the sale of fireworks and a crackdown on Public drunkenness."

Gibson wasn't satisfied.

"I thought you'd have a bigger perspective, Melia," he said. "You live in Manchester and this is Salford. Regional Office is in Salford. We need to know what's happening on our own doorstep! You can't even find the lost caskets - "

Melia thought that was a bit unfair too. Caulfield had been looking into that. She thought his trip to Irlam recently -

"I hate stories without endings," Captain Gibson said, his temper bubbling along underneath. "I wish we could tie a few ribbons around these latest happenings and just sign them off! I don't mean just filing a report and throwing it on my desk. I mean in Real Life. It's as frustrating as Afghanistan. We didn't finish anything there, we just left."

Melia looked at the man. His military bearing, his clipped moustache, he was probably missing his days in the Army, long ago when there were visible enemies and they could be defeated. Modern warfare didn't suit him at all.

"Melia," he said heavily, "this country is heading for a second Winter of Discontent. You're too young to remember the 1970s, but it was chaos. There was a shortage of fuel; electricity was off for some hours of the day; and shelves in the shops were often empty. Sound familiar? At that time it was about the huge hike in oil prices and discontent in the Trade Unions. What have we got now? A huge price rise in the price of gas and a workforce that is exhausted after eighteen months of pandemic and repeated Lock-downs. People are saying they're 'over worked and underpaid'. Snap. I've heard that before, but this year it's even worse than fifty years ago. Now we've got skill shortages and a population that won't stand for importing people to make up the gaps. They say it's all in the name of Brexit, but 2016 was a Referendum that promised 'freedom' and a better way of life, not shortages and rising prices. What we're currently experiencing is the reverse!"

Melia began to feel really, really uncomfortable. In all the years she had faithfully served the Captain she had never heard him even hint at disparaging politicians. They were Public Servants, for Heaven's sake! It didn't matter who was in power or what the crisis was, they had to serve their country, not criticise it!

Maybe Gibson was 'exhausted' and demoralised too. Maybe he was one of the discontents.

He said: "I don't have to list them for you, but it's everywhere. Everything. We've seen queues at petrol stations in the last few months. We've had domestic gas prices going up and small suppliers going out of business. The gas problem is affecting the gas-fired power stations and that cuts our supply of electricity. We've got a shortage of van drivers and lorry drivers, the people who are meant to distribute our food around the country, and we haven't enough pickers to take the vegetables out of the ground and the fruit from the trees. Thousands of migrant workers have packed up and left us to stew. They feel aggrieved and unwelcome. Why shouldn't they quit? We're even having problems taking rubbish away. Remind you of anything? In 1973 there were piles of black bags at every street corner. It was a mess."

Melia was twisting in her chair, not knowing which way to turn. Then she was rescued.

One of the kitchen volunteers came out of the Pavilion and started to clear their table. He asked, casually, if he could get them anything else, and Melia jumped at the chance. More tea, please, she asked politely.

Any distraction would do, to deflect her boss from his self-pitying descent into depression.

When the man came back with more drinks, this time on a tray, she decided to involve him in the discussion.

"What's your name?" she asked politely.

"Most people call me Mellors," he said, smiling at the attention.

"Sit down, sit down," she said. "We're just talking about the state of affairs in the country."

"I do need to take the weight off my feet," he said.

Gibson wasn't looking pleased at the interruption, but Melia persisted. This was Research, she was thinking.

"So, how's it going?" she asked him. "Really. Can you give us any insights?"

He obviously liked having some attention from this pretty woman. He was old enough to be her father, but he was a man, with the usual encumbrances. He wasn't above being flattered. His opinion? Sure, he had one.

He said: "Don't ask Dirk. You know Dirk Forrest? He's like the Head Honcho round here. He hasn't come in yet, he's got some other meeting. But people ask him your very question, and he always says, 'All good. All good.'"

Melia tried to smile. She was hoping that he would have had a view on the state of the world, to provide an alternative to the Captain. But the new man seemed more obsessed with the state of affairs closer to home.

"Let me tell you what you might not know," he said, confiding his important insights. "We get a lot of people in here, not just the allotment plot holders and the volunteers. Oh, sure, the City Choir comes in on a Thursday night, and that's nice, and there's the guitar players, singer songwriters and The Jane and Mike Band. But Dirk has put out a lot of invitations over this last summer. Back in school holidays we had the 'Birds of Prey' from Frodsham. The kids loved that."

"Sounds delightful," Melia said, encouragingly. What could possibly have gone wrong?

"They lost a couple," Mellors said heartily. "The darn buzzards just flew away."

"That's awful!"

"Then we had the 'EduRaptors' - lizards and snakes. The kids were screaming, terrified. Loving every minute."

"Problems?"

"Something got out. They wouldn't tell us what, but they said it might be living in the pond now."

Captain Gibson was either looking bored, or completely baffled. He had a more focussed approach.

"What about money?" he demanded.

"Oh, you heard about that?" the man answered. "The Committee came up with a plan to start a 'World Funding' bid. It wasn't for much, but it got off to a slow start, and then limped along for a while. I'm not sure they hit their target."

"Is that a problem?"

"The campaign has to include 'Rewards' for people who put in a certain amount of money. I'm not sure the Committee has put together enough seeds or plants to match their commitments. Darn, that would be embarrassing."

"The Mayor's here!" someone shouted, and the area suddenly got busy.

Sol Senate had turned up for a photo-opportunity, and was going around, shaking hands, posing for pics.

Captain Gibson knew exactly who he was but didn't want his own picture to be taken, so he got up out of his chair and stood in the shadows, behind the recycling bins.

Melia might have been equally discreet, but her niece Emma came in with the crowd, swept along by some people with guitars. Em knew musicians? Apparently. She helped them set up in the corner, by the hedge, then cleared space in the centre of the area outside the Pavilion. There was going to be -

Dancing.

Melia was feeling a little self-conscious. The last time she had danced - Well, there was the Ball, of course, but then there was the Country Dancing with Emma, Rumi and the Fair people.

As if to remind her, a chorus line of elves and fairies appeared, and stood along the fence like an Honour Guard.

Who invited them? Who invited anyone, she wondered, looked at the mish-mash of young and old?

Then Cyril Corsh swept in. He had a posse of men in suits behind him, but he personally seemed game for anything. He picked a partner and circled around in a kind of barn dance, the like of which Salford had never seen before.

Then Dirk arrived, finally, and unlocked the shipping container and started taking out all the tools - the spades, forks and hoes. He organised the volunteers to put them on their shoulders and stand in the background. Young men and women with cameras were snapping away, recording every moment on audio and video.

Cyril Corsh pushed to the front, picked up a spade from the pile on the ground and raised it.

Then he collapsed on the floor, writhing in agony.

"Don't go near him!" Captain Gibson bellowed, emerging from his lair. He recognised the symptoms of nerve agent poisoning, and knew that everyone was in danger. "Melia, form a cordon," he ordered her. "We need HazMat!"

Mellors saw an opportunity to be useful and directed all the other volunteers to ditch their tools, just in case. They piled them in the centre of the space. Everyone was worried, scared that they might have picked up something deadly.

An ambulance arrived and the paramedics were wearing protective gear. They had a trolley with them. They loaded Mr Cyril Corsh on board and wheeled him up the slope, with interested parties following on, chattering and looking anxious. Melia was in the throng. They arrived at the Manor House, and a helicopter was waiting in front, on the lawn.

"Thank Goodness for Air Ambulance," Melia remarked to Marilyn, who was standing there, looking on.

"Oh, that's Mr Corsh's own helicopter," Marilyn assured Melia pointedly.

She would recognise it anywhere.

Chapter Twenty Four: Favours

"Let's do a swap," Mr Smithers was suggesting to Lord Turnton.

The good Lord was suspicious. He had been out of sight for a good while recently, and the reason was that he was having problems 'at home', in Scotland. The land agent had told him that the bothy he was renting had been bought out by a property development company, and Turnton's lease was in the process of being 're-negotiated'.

He nearly fell off his chair when the Agent said that the property company was called Corsh Industries.

Now here he was, back in the North West of England, facing a man who said it was all his idea. Smithers had bought the little house and the parcel of land around it, and was preparing to use it in a complicated deal -

"It's simple," Smithers said, ingratiatingly. "I've got the Title Deeds to the property you're currently renting in Scotland. I'll hand them over to you, free and clear, if you put your name to this document assigning title of the Manor House."

Corsh Corporation had really been shaken up by the sudden appearance of Everley Bone and his millions, but Smithers - on behalf of all the Corsh family - was fighting back. He thought that if he swooped in and secured the Turnton claim to the old building, then he would have a significant new card to play in the game.

Mr Corsh was currently languishing in a coma in the nearby Salford Royal Hospital, attended by the finest doctors the National Health Service could provide. Mr Smithers was pained that all their money couldn't buy a higher standard of care, but there was no one in the Private Sector that understood nerve agent poisoning any better than the experienced local experts.

Smithers blamed himself. He should have been more forceful. He knew it was a mistake when Cyril started courting the Georgians and buying a stake in the oil business there. Corsh was a property company!

They didn't know anyone in Georgia! They couldn't speak the language. They were from Chicago. That was the market they knew and understood.

Even this arena of Salford -

Mr Smithers looked around. They were in the Conference Rooms, again. The Mayor Mr Senate, shamed by his voters into being more open and transparent about his support for the bidders involved in the Manor House deal, had agreed to a new Open Day. They were all there - the supermarket boss, the property developer from Ancoats, the Chinese guys.

In truth, Smithers was scared that they were losing it. He wanted an Ace-in-the-Hole for Team Corsh.

Lord Turnton was delivering a good performance of being the Reluctant Partner. Actually, he was thrilled by what was on the table. He looked eagerly at the Deeds. I'm going to sign these papers, and then I'm going to get out of town, he was promising himself. I'm going to high-tail it and head for the hills - before anyone else realises I'm not a Lord.

Smithers was telling him it was a 'win-win' bargain and they would both get what they wanted.

Mr Turnton doubted that. HE would get a good deal. Smithers? Not so much.

The large hall was starting to fill up. The place was laid out with large tables, large enough for ten people on each table. When Smithers had arrived, he had a table to himself. Now, people were encroaching on the other side.

They weren't business people! he was thinking. They were local residents. The Public!

He had no time for them.

"Well, all right," Turnton said, dragging it out. "I suppose I could agree to your new offer."

"The Terms have been modified as you required," Smithers assured him, trying to smile reassuringly.

He couldn't understand why the Lord hadn't brought his solicitor with him. That girl seemed to be on the ball. She was top notch. No, Turnton was flying solo. In some ways that made Smithers more confident that he could take him.

Lord Turnton put his name on the Transfer documents, then the Statement of Fact, assigning his claim to the Manor House, and finally the Declaration of Intent. It was a lot of paper, he was thinking. All good for recycling, later, when it was found to be worthless. He tried to hide his smile of contempt. These Americans, he was thinking! I win.

Turnton picked up all the papers that were his record, and stuffed them into an elegant briefcase. Then he granted Mr Smithers an elongated handshake and a brief smile and moved towards the exit as fast as he dared.

Mr Smithers picked up the one paper that he had left, the important one to him, and tucked it into the inside pocket of his jacket. I can leave too, he was thinking. I just need to go down and have a word with that Dirk Forrest guy, before I leave Buile Hill. The poisoned shovel was in his area, inside the fence. How on Earth had it got there, he wondered?

It was only minutes later that Mr Smithers was mugged.

He was in amongst the trees, heading downhill, and he didn't see the shadowy figure until the bigger man hammered him on the head and knocked him out.

It was the Woodcutter. He had been helped out that time by Lord Turnton, in the matter of freeing his children from the Magus, and he had promised the Lord he would repay him someday.

This was it. As he went through Mr Smithers's pockets, found the paper and removed it, the Woodcutter was thinking: my debt is repaid. I have made up for everything.

He had no idea why the Lord would want him to do the deed, but he was happy now it was done. Their bargain was over.

Now I am free, the Woodcutter thought, as he walked home.

* * * * *

Caulfield was in the general area, contributing to the smooth running of the day. But he wasn't in the Hall, he was outside the Depot, ensuring no stray kid or adventurer made it over the wall.

He needed to prevent another International Incident.

That kid who got shot, trespassing in the Depot - he was shot by American soldiers. If the Press got hold of that -

It was an Arms Store, sure, but not everyone realised it was a base owned and run by the USA. The Mayor had started a process of negotiation to get them removed, but it had taken the personal involvement of Captain Gibson and his team before any Government Minister was willing to hear the case for the Status Quo to be changed.

Eventually, a deal was hammered out. The Americans would be given a new site, closer to London. On that understanding, they confirmed they would be willing to evacuate their Salford base. Caulfield was there to ensure nobody witnessed the preparations. If anyone saw what was going on - well, there would be too many questions to answer.

The de-camp was essential, of course. The redevelopment of the Manor House and its environs couldn't possibly happen while there was still military equipment on site. The American Top Brass were willing to bring in heavy goods vehicles, under the cover of darkness, to rescue their fighting machines. Other equipment could be loaded into shipping containers and could come out by road. The lorries would be unmarked.

The Yanks were apologetic for any trouble they might have caused, locally. They said they would pay for the giant bonfire on Bonfire Night, but since that didn't happen, they simply brought up a lorry load of fireworks and told the Council to save it until New Year's Eve, or whenever was the most appropriate festive night around these parts.

They also offered to pay for a Guy to put on top of the bonfire, but when it came back from the Toy Workshop on Ordsall Lane, someone noticed it looked too much like Cyril Corsh, so the figure was put into store for later rebuild.

The main thing - really impressive - is that they said they would spend dollars to restore the historic wooden greenhouses at the southern end of the Depot, by the fence. The Mayor, and all his party, literally bit their hands off.

That was an offer the Council couldn't refuse.

* * * * *

After an hour or so, when Caulfield was getting cold and disconsolate, he was pleased to see Terry arrive.

The younger man offered to 'relieve him'. Terry would take over Depot duties. Caulfield had never felt so cheered up.

"Besides, I want you to show our new colleague around," Terry requested. "Have you met Bais? From America."

Richard Caulfield shook his head, slowly. No, he was pretty sure he hadn't. What was the catch?

Bais said: "I was here with Terry and Melia the first night, when the first shipment arrived. I'd like to see what's changed. Terry says you have the local knowledge."

Caulfield demurred. Who me? He tried to play it cool, but was secretly panicking. What would Bais ask him?

They were standing outside the Depot, and Bais turned left, walking down the slope and across the front of the Manor House. He seemed to know his way around this bit of Buile Hill, Caulfield was thinking.

He said: "Uh, we were in a car, over - there - and a van came in from - there - and started unloading."

Bais walked around the corner and was aware the door to the cellars was almost opposite the entrance to the Conference Rooms. He waited until he was sure no one was coming out or going in, then pulled out Terry's key.

"We have access," he said proudly.

He ushered Caulfield into the darkness, then switched on his torch as he closed the door behind them.

The Deputy Director nearly fell through the floor. Coffins? No! They'd gone to America, the drugs were processed -

Bais said: "Looks like the second delivery hasn't been collected yet."

The 'Second Delivery'? Caulfield was furious. No one had bothered to update him about this!

The agent called Bais lifted the lid on one casket, then probed around in the silk for evidence of drugs.

"The drugs are still there," he noted. "Good job we are staking this place out, waiting for the bad guys to collect."

Caulfield was at a loss. He knew nothing about it. Was this going to be a regular drug delivery route?

Luckily, Bais was happy to do all the talking. Seeing these boxes of death made him philosophical.

"You know," he said slowly, "none of this would be possible or even important if only the Americans could learn a little self-control. But, Oh No, they have to have immediate gratification. Anything to stave off the pangs of loneliness and failure. There's cocaine on Wall Street and opioids in the suburbs. It all started with the widespread use of cannabis in the 1950s and LSD in the '60s. Illegal drugs are eating away the heart of the nation. It's like addiction is endemic."

"Like alcohol in the 1920's?" Caulfield asked helpfully. "You got a stake in this?"

"My father was American," Bais admitted, "but mention it to anyone and I'll cut your throat."

Caulfield managed a weak smile. The man was joking?

He couldn't say much for his own country, Caulfield was thinking. The demand for chemicals was running wild in the UK too, but he had been told that the shipment in the first coffins was going abroad - to the USA.

Bais said, musing, "All right, I'm too religious for some of my colleagues, but I hate all these drugs. They're illegal for a reason, People! I really have no faith that Western civilisation will last another generation."

Caulfield stared. Was Bais predicting The End of Days?

Bais said: "Face it, comrade, we are policing Sodom and Gomorrah."

But the drug dealers -

Caulfield tried to frame his thoughts. He had been under the impression -

"Okay, look," he said, "the customers are in the USA. I get that. But aren't the suppliers their fellow countrymen? US invades Afghanistan in 2001, poppy production didn't go down, it went up. The Yanks were shipping dangerous chemicals back to their home turf, weren't they? The victims and the profiteers are the same blood, aren't they?"

Bais looked at him, as if he hadn't heard such an outlandish theory before. He smiled.

"Brother," he said quietly to Caulfield, "the drug pipeline from Afghan farms to American street corners is being controlled by the Russians. It's been there since the 1980s, (when they were the 'foreign invaders' in Afghanistan). Sure, good ol' USA arrived twenty years ago, but they couldn't even hold the native extremists at bay, let alone the established drugs trade."

But why? Caulfield was thinking.

If Americans wanted to sell cocaine to financial wizards on Wall Street, that was good old Capitalism -

Bais could see the Deputy Director's confusion.

"It's not Communism versus the world anymore," he said informatively. "We're all Capitalists now. But it is still the USA versus the rump of the USSR. Russia versus America. The Cold War continuing into this century!"

"You can't be serious - "

"A Tipping Point is looming," Bais said. "If enough Americans get hooked on drugs, then Russia has won."

"You seem almost pleased!"

Bais glared. "I've nothing good to say about Russians," he said. "They fight dirty. You know that nerve agent poison they spread on the spade handle for Cyril Corsh. It didn't kill him. He woke up from his coma. But he's got 'Locked In' syndrome. He can hear, he can think, but he can't speak or move his muscles voluntarily."

"That's horrible," Caulfield conceded. "It's like murder, but - "

"It's worse than death," Bais told him.

They both thought about that for a moment or two.

Then Bais said: "So, it's clear that the attack was a punishment. You have to ask yourself, what awful things has Mr Corsh from Chicago been up to that inspired his enemies to be so vicious and cruel? You see, I've worked in the US and I've seen Cyril in action, and I can tell you, he's no better than the thugs on the other side of the curtain."

There has to be a difference, Caulfield was thinking wildly. We're the Good Guys!

"You've met him, Mr Caulfield," Bais said quietly. "You're employed by TEEF. So tell me - your opinion - which heartless gang should you be supporting - the murderers and drug dealers from the USA or the equally horrible people from Russia?"

Chapter Twenty Five: Last Days

Melia was at home that evening, in her flat in Manchester, when there was a knock at the door.

"I've just got back," the bedraggled figure said, looking as if he was about to collapse.

"Come on in, Jordy," Melia said to her old Army colleague.

He looked awful. Matted hair, straggly beard, dirt on his face. Had he been sleeping rough?

His clothes were torn and streaked with dirt. No sign of a uniform. He looked good when clean, she was thinking.

"Afghanistan?" she asked quietly, trying to be helpful, reassuring.

He had slumped on the sofa. his arms splaying out, and the small rucksack he was carrying slipping to the floor. He was breathing heavy, as if he'd run up the stairs at full tilt, but that was impossible, Melia knew. His shortness of breath must have another cause. Illness? Covid? He was the shadow of the man she had served with.

"You want a drink?" she asked him. He was a 'brother in arms'. He could have anything he wanted, she was thinking.

"Coffee would be great," he said, his voice rasping.

"Something stronger?'

He smiled. "I haven't touched alcohol for nearly a year. Sorry to disappoint you, Mels, but I'm not the hell-raiser I once was. I've lost a lot of weight and my stamina is shot, completely. I've had a bad journey."

She let him slump back. I might have to steam clean the fabric, she was thinking wryly. Not to worry.

Melia came back with a tray. There was coffee in a pot, so he could serve himself. There were biscuits on a plate, and some fruit, all she had, served Middle Eastern style. They had dined together more than once. She knew his tastes.

"You need a place to stay?" she asked quietly, once the coffee was going down.

He smiled again. "A roof over my head would be a welcome change," he admitted. "But that's not why I'm here. I caught the goss on the grapevine that you were running point on the coffin delivery. That right?"

Melia was stunned. How on Earth did he know that? Still, she wouldn't lie to him. They were pals.

Jordy suddenly put his cup back on the tray. She could see his hands were shaking. He had it bad.

He said: "I've come a long way since I was Sergeant Jordy Faulkner. I'm out and I'm back. You don't owe me anything, Mels, but I'd sure be glad of your help in this little matter. A friend of mine was in those boxes."

Melia was horrified. A 'friend' of his? Would he want to know what happened to the body? Would he be expecting a formal burial? That's what a serving officer might be entitled to. That, and a recording of the time and place.

How could Melia possibly explain what actually went on and where the bodies were disposed of? Melia had read Caulfield's report, and it was a horror story. Nobody deserved to be treated that way! Nobody.

Jordy asked: "Where were the bodies buried?"

Melia hesitated, but she could supply an answer to that assumption, she realised.

"They were cremated," she stated. I can tell him more later, when he's rested, she was thinking.

In fact, Caulfield, acting totally out of character, had gone up to the Woodland Cemetery in Wardley and got permission from the Bishop himself to scatter the ashes amongst some newly planted trees in the converted meadow. It had a lovely view.

'The ashes' were whatever remnants he could recover from the old steel mill site. Some of the white stuff was probably human, but it was mixed in with all sorts of ash and effluent. The less said about that, the better.

"What about the coffins?" he asked quietly.

What an odd question, Melia was thinking! Wouldn't everyone assume that if there was a professional cremation, then the caskets would simply go in the furnace. Why would Jordy think that might not happen?

He explained.

"We all knew the boxes were expensive," he said. "The agreement was that once they arrived in England, they could be swapped for something cheaper, maybe wicker, and then the money made would pay for the actual funerals."

Melia nodded. Well, something like that did happen, she knew. The caskets were re-purposed and sold to the USA.

"What about the drugs, Mel?"

Melia stared at her old pal. He knew about the drugs? He knew that the whole coffin project was a thinly disguised way of smuggling drugs out of the country? Melia shook herself. She'd assumed that Jordy was an innocent bystander.

"I put them in there, Mels." he said simply. His voice was now steady, his eyes steely and bright.

Melia knew the drugs had been cleaned out, but then tracked down by the unlikely figure of Caulfield, who found the gunk being processed in his own backyard. He'd tipped off Major Crimes and they'd raided the premises. By that time, Caulfield had put his flood-prone house on the market and was now living in North Salford, not far from Mickey's house.

"It was well worked-out plan," he said. "We knew we faced a gloomy future. What was there for us back here - a small pension, a medal or two, but nothing public, in case the real history of what we got up to came out. So we all chipped in and bought and stole as many kilos as we could, stuffing them in the caskets. Then, me and Lionel headed north, to lay a trail for the authorities and lead them off the track. They were so busy chasing us, they didn't see the plane leave."

Melia drew a heavy breath. Jordy was talking about breaking laws, theft - and who knew what else?

"Did you get out of the country?" she asked quietly.

He shook his head, bitterly.

"We drove a long way, but local warlords wouldn't let us through their territory. Then we walked. Then we got separated. I was picked up by a tribe that had supplied some of the material we had stolen in Kabul. They didn't like me. I was tortured for a while. When they got bored, they sold me to the Russians."

Melia thought she was worldly-wise, but this was far too way-out even for her experience and expertise.

"What - what happened then?"

"Oh, that bit was easy," Jordy chuckled. "I just had to play awkward for a while, and then cave in and pretend that I'd be happy to spy for them. That changed everything. They were happy to pay for me to be passed along the chain to Germany, and they put me on a flight back to Manchester. The tricky bit was disappearing then, going underground so they couldn't find me. Or the Army. Or anyone else, like Border Force. So here I am. No one knows I'm here. But now you know, Mels. Just you."

Melia was again lost for words. After a minute, she asked: "Jordy - did you desert ?"

He chuckled. "That's the smallest thing I've done wrong," he agreed, "and not the worst. Basically, I've been fighting my way out, all the way from Afghan. But listen, I'm rich, right? Someone has got that product. It's mine."

Melia looked around, desperately. How could she distract him? More coffee?

He said: "Melia, the team got the message, right? You knew the drugs were in there. You knew I was going to be calling on one of you, sooner or later. I didn't know it was you, of course, but thought I could trust Captain Gibson."

"You told Gibson your plan?" Melia gasped, uncomprehendingly.

"Sure. I knew I could trust him. He owes me a few favours."

Melia stood up, flustered.

Her boss was told Jordy's hare-brained scheme? But he hadn't mentioned it to anyone - not her, not Caulfield, the drone who had been chasing his tail to find the 'drug smugglers', the mystery men. Gibson knew who they were?

Jordy was uncoiling himself from his laid-back position. Suddenly, he was sitting up straight.

"Melia? Melia, come on! You're giving me goosebumps," he said. "What is it you aren't telling me?"

The poor girl felt as though she was in shock. All the revelations. Melia's world was being turned upside-down.

Then, an even more troubling thought occurred to her.

"It was a good plan," she told her friend, nodding and smiling at him. "So you did it again?"

He looked at her as though she was completely mad. He was shaking his head in bafflement.

"No, only one go," he told her. "There was enough money there to set us up for life, when we got back here."

"But it did happen again,' she told him. "Another delivery, exactly the same as the first."

"But that - that could only mean - "

He sat back again, and his head was in his hands. It was as though the life was being sucked out of his body.

"There is only one way that could happen," he said quietly, "and that's if the guys who were helping us decided it was a good pipeline and started using it for their own ends. And that would only work if they bribed people - "

He stared at Melia, and his face was white.

"They sold us out. They tipped you off, didn't they?"

Melia considered. Of course, there was that. Why was she outside the Manor House? Because of a tip-off!

"I'm dead," he whispered. "I've got no family, no friends. I was relying on the cash I'd make - "

"What about Lionel?"

"He didn't make it."

Jordy was suddenly silent. He had nothing to say. The plan he had come up with was to save his life, get him out of where he'd been and launch him into a whole new future. Now, he saw, there was none of that.

It was all over.

"Jordy, I'm sorry," Melia began, but he wasn't listening.

Slowly, imperceptibly, Jordy worked his way to the edge of the sofa and draped one languid hand over the edge. He pulled up his small bag and dumped it into his lap. He worried at the latches and opened the top.

Melia realised, in one awful moment, precisely what he had in mind - and she wasn't having it.

"Jordy, there's no need for that - " she said, her voice rising.

He had pulled out a small revolver and was checking the chambers.

Here? In my apartment? Melia gasped, and was suddenly very angry. He'd been her friend! Did he think that was gone?

"Jordy," she told him, "I'm not going to let you do it."

He wasn't even looking at her. His eyes were down and both his hands were full of the gun. He was toying with it.

"No," Melia told him firmly. "No, Jordy. No. You are not - "

She leapt forwards and landed on him. Her weight dragged him to the floor and they rolled on the carpet.

There was a single shot.

THE END

ABOUT THE AUTHOR

What can you say about Mike Scantlebury -

that hasn't been turned written on the subway walls?

(Leaving out the Army record, and the first album -)

Well, he says he was born in a sure fired hurricane but it's all right now. He transferred to England when quite young, toddling, and not able to chase anything. His family settled in the West Country of England, near a quiet suburb of a noisy town, where his father, a gifted ventriloquist, talked to people without them noticing. When face to face communication became the norm in the 1980s, Mike packed a cat and dog and squatted with ex-student friends in the big city of Bristol. This is where he first purchased a ukulele, stole a guitar, inherited a case and took it to the courts.

You can find Mike Scantlebury on the internet.

It's @MikeScantlebury[1] on Twitter and 'mikescantlebury99[2]' on Facebook. And, surprise, 'mikescantlebury[3]' on Linked In.

If you want to see Mike singing and spitting, try Youtube.

https://www.youtube.com/user/mikescantlebury[4]

---

1.   https://twitter.com/MikeScantlebury

2.   https://www.facebook.com/mikescantlebury99

3.   https://www.uk.linkedin.com/in/mikescantlebury

4.   https://www.youtube.com/user/

mikescantlebury?ob=0&feature=results_main

If all else fails, try him at home (he's sometimes in, or in the garden): http://www.Salford.me/

Other Books by Mike Scantlebury

(Author of Scanti-Noir)

The 'Amelia Hartliss Mysteries' series
Book One: Poison Doctor
Book Two: Hartliss Running
Book Three: Prince William (At Olympics 2012)
Book Four: Con-Fusion
Book Five: Mayors' Tales
Book Six: Secret Garden Festival 2012
Book Seven: Kidnapping Cameron
Book Eight: Secret Garden 2013
Book Nine: Fresh Heir
Book Ten: The Golden Chip
Book Eleven: The Folksinger 2013
Book Twelve: Salford World War
Book Fourteen: Salford Trenches
Book Fifteen: Terror Beach
Book Sixteen: A Shot at Mayor
Book Seventeen: JC's Cure for cancer
Book Eighteen: Arms it is
Book Nineteen: People say stuff
Book Twenty: Everybody Lies
Book Twenty One: Co-Vid2020
Book Twenty Two: Co-Vid2020, Part Two
Book Twenty Three: Co-Vid2020, Part Three
Book Twenty Four: Co-Vid2020, Part Four

The 'Mickey from Manchester' series

Book One: Black and White

Book Two: Off The Rails

Book Three: A Limp Piccolo

Book Four: Filling In

Book Five: New, Clear Future

Book Six: Housing Erases Debts

Book Seven: The Bone Key Curse

Book Eight: Multimedia (*BBC comes to Salford*)

Book Nine: Lucky Ignatius

Book Ten: Reverend Dumb

Book Eleven: Jennercide

Book Twelve: Lethal Election

Book Fourteen: Trumps A Mayor

Book Fifteen: Senctioned

Book Sixteen: 75 Years

Book Seventeen: Globoil Marxits

Book Eighteen: Global Markets, Part 2

Book Nineteen: The Great British FAKE Housing Crisis

Book Twenty: Housing Crisis, Part 2

Book Twenty One: Housing Crisis, Part 3

Book Twenty Two: Housing Crisis, Part 4

Book Twenty Three: Korruption Kills

Book Twenty Four: Korruption Kills, Part 2

Note: That's 'Mickey from Manchester', is it?

Well, he may be 'FROM' Manchester, but he certainly doesn't live there anymore.

Oh, and his name isn't 'Mickey', really.

Don't miss out!

Visit the website below and you can sign up to receive emails whenever Mike Scantlebury publishes a new book. There's no charge and no obligation.

https://books2read.com/r/B-A-SODI-FQFMC

BOOKS 2 READ

Connecting independent readers to independent writers.

Also by Mike Scantlebury

Amelia Hartliss Mysteries
People Say Stuff
Everybody Lies
Co-Vid 2020
Co-Vid 2020, Part 2
Tales Of Old Buile Hill

Mickey from Manchester Series
The Great British Fake Housing Crisis, Part 1
The Great British Fake Housing Crisis, Part 2
Korruption Kills, Part 2

Mickey Starts
Never Say Di
"It's Maurice. See?"
Bann The Bomber
"You Knighted Killers, Ma'am"
The Chinese Connection
New Man
Still Waters

Watch for more at www.Salford.me.

About the Author

Mike Scantlebury is a name that's hard to remember, but it's impossible to forget. Inspired by Scandinavian thrillers he has created a line of crime and espionage novels he likes to call 'Scanti-Noir'. That's unique in Britain, or at least, rare, in the North West of England where he lives. It's a land famous for football clubs, pop singers, bad weather and TV dramas, but Mike gets his ideas from the narrow streets and wide minds he encounters every day. There's not a stone he hasn't looked under, or a new leaf he hasn't turned over. Whatever happens in the book you're reading, beware - there's more where that came from!

Read more at www.Salford.me.

About the Publisher

Rosewood Press started in 1993, and was a new business re-launching an old and respected name. Rosewood Partners started a range of titles, including Romance, Crime Fiction, Mysteries, Thrillers and Science Fiction. Mike Scantlebury, author, came forward with a range of Romance titles, based around the heroines Amelia Hartliss, (Melia, known to her friends and lovers as 'Heartless') and the young ladies of the Farley Family. Some of the projected novels never made it past the planning stage, and this is what these books are. 'Romantic Beginnings' are just the first few chapters of novels that never got finished. Luckily, most had a plot worked out, which is why a 'Synopsis' is included where appropriate.

Don't forget: it's never too late. If you want to know the end of the story, just write in. Rosewood Ramblings will consider asking their authors to complete the 'Beginnings' included here - but only by popular demand! Make your preferences clear!

Milton Keynes UK
Ingram Content Group UK Ltd.
UKHW012329110823
426770UK00001B/1